DESTROYED BY
'ISHQ'..

DESTROYED BY
'ISHQ'..

When love defies your very being...

Mr. Invisible

Srishti
PUBLISHERS & DISTRIBUTORS

Srishti Publishers & Distributors
N-16, C. R. Park
New Delhi 110 019
editorial@srishtipublishers.com

First published by
Srishti Publishers & Distributors in 2013

Typeset by Eshu Graphic

To my friend who was very much unlike me.

I want to know
Whether you remember me
Like I remember you,
I want to know
Whether you care for me
Like I care for you,
I want to know
Whether I live in you
Like you live in me,
I want to know
Whether you love me
Like I love you,
I want to know
Whether you'd die for me
Like I died for you,
I want to know
Whether you will be mine
Like I'm yours...

FOREWORD

WAIT! LISTEN TO ME FIRST...

Alright, now that you're holding this book in your hands, I must ask you two very important questions:

1. What bugs you the most in life?

2. Who is your biggest enemy?

For most of you the answers to both the above questions must be simple to imagine but difficult to state and justify.

Let's get you some help. Why don't you write this down in the space below...

C'mon, it isn't such a big deal. Just pick up a pen and fill these two coloumns -

PROBLEMS	ENEMIES

Now, take a deep breath and tell yourself -

"Yes, I have the ability to overcome all problems in life."

Say that aloud. Say that to your closest friend. Say it over and over again.

Now tell yourself -

"I have no enemies. I am made to love, not to hate. I love everyone."

Say that aloud. Keep repeating it.

Doesn't it feel better? I bet it does...

Life is only as complicated as we make it. There is a solution to everything in life and the solution lies in being able to understand the problem and talk about it.

Is there anything you want to say someone? Is there something you're holding back because you're worried of the consequences?

Life is short, and so you need to act fast. Don't waste time in thinking about it, just go ahead and do it!

You might not get another chance.

If you love someone, let them know! Call them now... If a call isn't possible, send a small text message. Do anything, just don't hold your feelings back!

I wish you the best of everything! Now you may read the book...

BARE BEGINNINGS...

It was the 11th day of the 2nd annual 'Hacking season'. I was enjoying the evening coffee while watching 'A beautiful mind' in my cozy chamber. Rick had just left the room as he wanted to *study* something. He was my best friend. I had confided the best of my secrets to him. I and Rick were the only two people for whom this month long hacking season really held any meaning. It was an exciting festival for us, which we celebrated together in B/501 – my hostel room which Rick calls 'The Hacking Headquarters'. A deep feeling of revenge had impregnated this idea in my mind, exactly one year ago. It was simple. For the whole year, we would keep listing down names of people who have been irritating us and then, during the hacking season, we would take over their online presence completely. This meant laying hands over their E-mail and social networking accounts and any other related accounts. We just had one policy – we wouldn't do any damage to anyone's real life. We would simply seize an account, keep a copy of all its data, and leave it once we felt the necessary lesson was learnt by the victim by merely being over-concerned about his accounts. 'It helps them take better care of their accounts in future', as Rick would justify. He loved the seasons nonetheless.

This time, Rick and I had already laid hands over 91 Google Mail accounts, 108 Yahoo! Accounts, 267 Facebook accounts and several paid subscriptions to file sharing sites, adult dating sites, and what not! It was only yesterday evening that something bad happened and we had to concentrate our efforts towards one single person. It was a tough job, and so I had to take a small movie-break to calm down. Rick, however, was still busy with something. As I was being mesmerized by the aroma of the brewing espresso, my Nokia 3310 beeped, indicating an incoming message –

We need your services urgently, pls rush to room no.
706, Block G

I kept the phone back on my desk. I was well aware what the case might be, and tried not to get over-excited. I had no first-hand knowledge about the scenario, and it seemed like the only opportunity for me to find out what was the real issue behind all the controversial things that had been happening since yesterday. I rose from my chair, placed the empty coffee cup neatly upon the table, and turned to my laptop. I checked my encrypted portable hard-drive to make sure I wasn't missing any useful software which might be helpful, and then slipped it into my side-bag which also contained my camera, a notepad, and a very useful toolbox with more than a hundred kinds of screw-driver attachments. I couldn't risk carrying my laptop, as it contained material which could've fuelled many other controversies, much more complicated than the one that I was about to witness.

As I opened the door of my 110-sq. feet hacking headquarters, I found Rick still tensed and making notes on his laptop. He looked disturbed.

"Don't you think a little rest won't do any harm," I asked him knowing that he had barely slept the previous night.

He smiled wryly and said, "I find it really difficult to believe it was a suicide."

"Yes. But we need some strong evidence before the situations get out of hand," I asserted.

I wondered if we were treading along the right path or not. It was risky. "Let's see what the night has hidden, that the morning shall unveil," I quipped.

He gave me a puzzled look when he realized that I was getting ready to go somewhere.

"Mysteries calling!" I said as I left Room No. B/501

♡ ♡ ♡

I took my Canon camera out of my bag and held it tightly, as I always do, in my right hand. The lift door opened at the seventh floor. Several policemen greeted me with suspicious looks. On any given day, I can look more like a terrorist than a typical computer freak. As if my dense, unshaved-since-months, beard, uncombed hair, and bathroom slippers were not enough, the small camera in my hand drove them further into suspicion. I put my right hand inside the side-bag that swayed on my right, hiding the camera, and tried to avoid the smirk some of them sported as I moved towards Room No. 706, which was the office of some insane algorithms professor at IIT.

I entered the centrally air-conditioned room. There was complete silence. Rony and DKP raised their heads to look at me. Bhalu resumed crying. They were *his* friends. They all had their real names, of course, which were forgotten in the last one and a half years in IIT. Ronit Bansal became Rony – an asshole all the way, Dhirendra Kapur became DKP – a die-hard romantic, and the only one amongst them who failed to get a fancy nickname was Avinash Baruda aka *Bhalu* (meaning 'bear'), who hasn't yet learnt how to use his brain. Of all them, Rony seemed to be the most calm and composed character that day even though everyone else was tensed. *Very much unlike him*, I noted mentally.

Two professors looked at me with hope. The only other professor in the room was busy talking on the phone in a lonely corner of the room. A police officer was standing near the professors with his eyes intently fixed on a laptop which was, possibly, Aarav's.

I was just about to speak something when the talkative professor in the lonely corner ended his phone call and spoke,

"So you're that all-knowing hacker…"

"I am sorry sir, but I'm not a hacker," I tried to divert his mind. I really didn't understand how they even got the hint of my capabilities. I didn't want to expose my activities…

"Ok, whatever. But these guys think you are the perfect person who can help us at the moment," said the old professor, with a serious look. Without waiting for me to enquire anything he added, "There was a suicide note on Aarav's laptop. His friend Dhirendra, here, was asked to copy it to the pen-drive..."

Everyone looked at DKP. He took a deep breath and gave a blank expression. The professor continued, "...but he accidentally did shift-delete, instead of control-c..."

I couldn't help smiling. While pressing the 'Ctrl' key along with the letter 'C' meant copying a file, pressing 'Shift' and 'Delete' keys together was a well-known shortcut for deleting the selected file permanently, without moving it to the Recycle bin first. *How could a computer science student ever do such a silly mistake?* I wondered.

"Now you have to get that file back, or these guys can be in big trouble," concluded the professor.

It was no big deal for me. Moreover, it could give me an opportunity to get hold of the suicide note and keep it for myself – who knows what can be useful in future. Nobody knew why he had committed suicide. Some even believed it was a murder. I was neutral regarding this as I had no evidence. Moreover, I always feel information is the biggest weapon and must be used wisely and at the perfect time.

Without waiting for any further instructions, I moved near the laptop and began analyzing it. Although I knew it was easy for me, I tried to sound confused because otherwise it would've proved in front of everyone that I am actually a hacker. I think only DKP had some hint. As the recovery process began, one of the professors asked me if the file could really be recovered once it was shift-deleted. Morons all of them – They still call themselves professors…

"There's going to be some interesting news in the newspapers tomorrow, the media is excited to know what the ten-page suicide note contained," exclaimed another professor. He was trying his best to keep calm and allow the minimum amount of disclosure to the media. He also asked the police if Kaavya could go home.

"We need to interrogate the girl, let her not leave the hostel; this is usually the case with today's generation. They don't understand the importance of life, giving too much importance to love…" said the horrible looking police officer.

Whatever they were talking was extremely confusing to me. Kaavya, from what I last knew, was Aarav's girlfriend. I didn't know what had happened since yesterday. So the only option was to wait and find out what was written in the suicide note. It was going to take several hours to scan a whole four hundred gig (Gigabyte, GB, that's how we say it) hard drive. So I left room no. 706, and tried to find a quiet place to think about and note down whatever I had just sensed. I sat on the floor, not too far from the area where there was too much depression and sadness in the air, but far enough so that nobody could find me. I opened my spare diary, and began noting down the happenings since yesterday in the highest amount of detail that I could. While I was deeply engrossed, Rony came up and said, "please don't become a psycho, we've already witnessed Aarav become one…even if your diaries get destroyed, don't lose your calm." I had absolutely no idea what he was talking about. I kept on looking at him, as he disappeared...

Rony is an asshole all the way. It is something that doesn't require any evidence. Yet he never fails to put up one. So I usually ignore his remarks.

It suddenly struck me that none of the three guys – Rony, DKP or Bhalu – had even attended the funeral which was going on right at that very moment. They, reportedly, hadn't stayed at the hospital last night, where Aarav's body was lying unattended. The room was locked from outside, but not from inside, when the suicide happened; and now that deleted suicide note. Situations didn't indicate positive things.

I went back to the laptop to see the progress of the recovery process. I was almost dumbfounded when I saw a whole 9 MB RAR archive named 'MY LIFE' getting recovered. They said it was a suicide note, but something made me feel Aarav had left more than a suicide note. I copied the recovered contents into my hard drive which was already connected, without letting anyone know. Information is the biggest weapon...

"I think it's better to leave this matter with the forensic department, I don't think we are going to find that file," were my last words to the police officials. What if it was really a murder...*No, it is not possible* – I tried to console myself. The next moment, I found myself walking towards the hostel, far away from Block G. I had to ask Rick about his findings and let him know what I was feeling. Maybe he was right. Maybe it was not suicide after all...

A DAY AGO...

The time was ten minutes to five in the evening. Rick was sitting next to me and we were working on an article. He was too busy as he was also trying to even up with the current boyfriend of his long time crush by taking over his Facebook account, in my room – which had been the headquarters for all such activities for more than a year. Rick was one of his kind Facebook demolisher. He was physically not very strong, but made up for his physical inabilities by being great in the cyber-world. He was completely aware of the latest cyber laws in most countries of the world; obviously his techniques were, in good amount, replicas of my own.

Suddenly, Rick stood up from his chair, yawned a bit, took a sip from his can of coke and declared, "I think I need to stretch my muscles a bit..."

We had been working since afternoon. Even I was feeling sluggish. So I agreed and said, "Yeah, let's go to the gym"

We came out of the room and had barely reached near the staircase when I noticed that several students were running towards the ground floor. Another thing that was common among all of them was that they all were apparently sad and dumbfounded. We felt something was wrong. Just then, Vicky stumbled upon me. There was fear and surprise in his eyes.

"Hey Vicky, what's the matter?" Rick enquired.

Vicky looked exasperated, and spoke, "Aa...Aarav has... committed suicide..."

He was breathing heavily. Without waiting for our reaction, he rushed towards the ground floor.

Needless to say, I and Rick were dumbfounded too. It was unbelievable. We stood there, in silence. Then without waiting for another moment we ran towards Aarav's room which was on the ground floor. I was walking slowly towards that corridor, where a lot of people were standing, completely horrified. The whole environment was too gloomy. I gathered some courage to move closer to Aarav's room. Dhirendra and Avinash lay slumped against the ground, crying their hearts out. Several officials and guards had gathered around the room, in which there lay a broken chair, the strangled body of Aarav and two neatly placed suitcases. The room had been locked from outside and they had to break it open, as it was evident from the condition of the lock. Some people entered and tried to lift him, but he was probably gone...

Everyone was appalled by the sight of Aarav – he wasn't even completely dressed. In times when the temperature used to drop to as low as five degrees, he was still wearing only one outer t-shirt and shorts.

I asked Rick to stay there and I came back to my room and tried to do the usual checks with Aarav's E-mail and

Facebook accounts to see if I could get any clues. Amazingly, his Facebook account had been deactivated. I reckoned that he had done the same thing with his Gmail too. My brain stopped thinking for a while. I tried to concentrate and find a way, but the internet connection was lost. Weird, wasn't it? Somehow, I found information, from previously stored records, about his parents, his native place, etc. But that information was not really useful.

I cancelled all evening tasks, except dinner... I was somewhat frightened.

Aarav, our batch-mate in the computer science department, was a rather juvenile guy. His home was not far away from the university. He had scored 9.6 on the pointer scale in the last semester at the university. He wasn't one of those book worms as I knew him. His suicide came across as a completely unexpected event. Nobody could understand what his problems were. I am not very close to any of his group guys, and so I cannot say if there were any personal issues that might have disturbed him. He used to be in a jolly mood, since first year, although he had been very quiet and inactive for the last few months. I couldn't believe this had actually happened. Had I not seen the hanging body, I would not have believed it.

The next twenty hours were spent, completely unsure about what to do. There was horror, suspense, doubt, anxiety and mental disturbance. At 4pm, the next day, it was his funeral. Everyone was supposed to gather there, out of humanity at least. I and Rick were informed by Rony about it. "You guys reach there, we have an important meeting with Prof. Thakur and will come later." were Rony's words. Maybe the three guys – DKP, Rony and Bhalu – were being interrogated, or maybe they were just not allowed to leave the university premises. They were his closest friends and neighbors in the hostel. Whatever might have been the reason, I and Rick had no time to think about it. I was of the opinion that someone should stay back at the hostel in case some urgent need arose. Who knew when we might need to track someone's Facebook activity or hack someone's E-mail account! With almost everyone else determined to go, I felt it was best if I and Rick stayed back at the hostel.

We came back to my room. To loosen the grip of weary feelings, I began preparing coffee while watching 'A beautiful mind'. It was ten minutes after this that my cellphone beeped...

BACK TO HOSTEL...

Icame back from Block G, and met Rick right away. "I don't find their reactions in tune with the happenings," I snapped my point of view. "Exactly MI, I've found some very contrasting features about the whole incident." He called me MI, pronounced 'em eye', sometimes. It was his way of shortening my rather long and unusual name – Mr. Invisible. He showed me a small document on his laptop:

- Where is the person who locked the room from outside? And who is he?

- How can the room not be locked from inside?

- How could they find it out immediately from the ventilator, that he had hanged himself?

- Why were his friends not present at the funeral, or even at the hospital?

- Everyone was so afraid, what can be the reason?

- A digital suicide note (innovative), although Aarav wasn't known to be able to type much.

- 'Ctrl+x' becomes 'Shift+Delete': Illogical and unexplainable.

- Rony's carefree behavior at that time and his unexplained absence from the hostel at the time when the incident took place.

"Are you trying to say, it is a staged suicide incident?" I just wanted to confirm. "Somewhat...," was all Rick could say. I could sense trouble.

If some people and newspapers are to be believed, it is being said that Aarav had been missing only since morning that day – hardly something to worry about. His friends, knowing his Gmail password, tried to log in and find out whom he had been talking to. But he had changed his password more than six hours ago, at that time. So they felt they could get into his room, take his laptop, and log into Gmail, as it would have his saved passwords. It was when they tried to enter through the ventilator that the hanging body of Aarav was seen. Everyone got frightened and ran for help.

Aarav's relatives were reportedly furious seeing that nobody from the university administration came to the funeral; and not even from the group which Aarav belonged to. Maybe his parents knew about Kaavya. Such things don't remain hidden for long.

I couldn't sleep the whole night. There were a lot of things that I was thinking about. This included my own encounters with Aarav during our early months at the university. He was a very friendly guy and always used to crack intelligent jokes. Everything flashed in front of my eyes. I couldn't believe he was so serious in his relationship, with Kaavya, that it could be a reason for killing himself. But I didn't want to come to any conclusions so easily. Almost past midnight, I recalled about the 'MY LIFE' folder that I had secretly copied onto my hard drive. I called Rick immediately. The next moment, I opened my laptop, and began searching for it. It was there – a 9.3 MB folder, containing a lot of text documents, some web-pages and some pictures. My heart-beat was increasing, as I was uncertain about the ramifications of my secret study. There were a lot of files in that folder. I double-clicked on a file named 'final decision.txt' and waited for the file to open. A couple of seconds later, it was still opening. It shouldn't have taken so long for a 2 KB text file to open. I tried to extract the whole archive but, alas, it was corrupted. I tried to open each file, but none of them opened. I was becoming impatient. I was about to frown over my own inefficiency – but nothing was in my hands.

"Yes, did you find something MI?" Rick asked me as soon as I opened the door of my room and let him in. He had brought his laptop with him. I narrated the whole incident, my observations and everything else.

"Maybe we should wait for some time and see how things unfold," Rick suggested. While leaving, Rick mentioned that DKP, Rony and Bhalu were staying in some other rooms, as their rooms had been locked for inspection.

I spent the remainder of that night, completely restless, the names of the various files revolving all around in my thoughts...

NEXT DAY: Sorry Rony...

Soon the morning sun showed its hood. I hadn't slept. I couldn't have slept.

"The three guys are staying in the next lobby. And they've got some E-mails from Aarav..." informed Rick. He usually comes to wake me up, but that day he didn't have to try much – I was already awake.

"Who's got mails?" I enquired.

"I am not sure but maybe it's Rony," said Rick.

Alright. Here I was both tensed and excited. I had lost that precious 9 MB thing, but now there was an opportunity to get some or all of the material back. And that required me to do something I wasn't in the mood for. For a moment I was quiet. Rick sensed the meaning of my silence and spoke,

"C'mon, it's no big deal."

To be frank, we hardly cared about Aarav being alive or dead, or maybe Rick cared a little but I didn't. It made no sense to us, because we had our own world to care about. It was 8 am, and without thinking further we began the process to add two more achievements to the second annual hacking season – one, Rony's Gmail account, and two, some suicide-note sort of thing which could help us simplify the confusion over Aarav's suicide.

Now hacking is not all that fun to do. It involves a lot of risk. The moment it becomes possible to trace your identity, the game is over. You always have to keep balancing between stupid victims and complicated internet rules. However, we had different approaches for different situations.

It was a simple thing to hack into Rony's account. Simpler than what we had thought. His security question was ALSO about love...

"It's simple you know. It says, 'First Love'..." said Rick, "Do we know his first love?" he asked me.

We knew Rony and his exhibitionist nature. We also knew he was dumb to the core. We had witnessed his nonsensical talks and his failed quest for love for more than a year. What happened next was just another proof. Hadn't I said he never fails to prove his dumbness?!

I entered a name in the box meant for the answer to that security question and hit 'Submit'. The next page gave us the option to reset his password. Rick smiled at me, demanding an explanation.

"I'll tell you that later. Change his password first and get some interesting information out..." I said.

"Umm...let's see...yes, that would be great as his new password!" Rick wrote something as the new password and turned towards me for a response.

"Yeah, be quick. And just remember whatever you set as his password because we might need it later. And also update our records with this data. One more victim…" I told him.

Rony's Gmail account opened. I immediately began searching. I was looking for words such as 'Aarav', 'suicide' and 'My life'. We didn't have much time before Rony found out and changed his password. I was becoming more and more conscious with each passing second. What if we didn't find anything? We would have to try out DKP's account, if Rony's would turn out to be vague. I had done it once and it would be more difficult to get hold over DKP's mails one more time. To my amazement, the 9.3 MB RAR archive was there. It was a forwarded message from DKP. I downloaded it instantly, and logged out. Now we would know what the truth was. We had slight hints about Kaavya, but the contents of this archive must make it sure. The archive contents were getting extracted, and it increased my excitement, and lowered my restlessness…

TOO MUCH TO READ...

It didn't take much time to extract the archive. Once the extraction process was complete, Rick opened the extracted folder named 'My Life' and began reading out –

"Ok, 'decisive me', 'final decision', 'songs', 'untold and unsaid'...that's lot of stuff to read...I can't believe he wrote all that," he said, looking at the files in that folder.

I looked at the computer screen. There were some folders and a lot of text files. On close inspection, I also found a picture. It was Kaavya's photograph. I really get pissed off by these things. So I closed the photo viewer which showed her photograph and yawned. I had lost all interest in reading that stuff – partly because of its quantity and partly because of the theme – Love.

"That's too much to read," I said, still yawning. Rick looked at me in dismay. Maybe he was interested in reading it. Even I was, a little, but I was too tired because of not sleeping the last night. I stood up from my chair, went up to my bed and lay down for short nap.

"Don't tell me you'll fucking sleep now," said Rick, a little amused. The F-word is a necessary ritual for him. He needs it badly to get things going. If he isn't using the F-word, you can say he isn't really serious.

"Yeah I will! You read that crap and tell me the story when I wake up, OK?"

Actually Rick has this uncanny ability to narrate stories in the first person. He builds the story, picks up his favorite character and begins narrating from the perspective of that character. Sometimes I feel he has some kind of Dissociative Identity Disorder, but he's perfectly normal when not telling stories.

Without waiting for his reply I fell asleep. The last thing I saw was Rick, sitting on the chair, with his eyes glued to the large computer screen. I must say he is a good reader as well…

"MI…dude…wake up!" Rick shouted.

I woke up, gasping for breath and looked straight at the door. It was closed, locked and intact. I then looked at the computer. It was intact too. I don't know why, but while sleeping I always have this fear that someone will, someday, break open the door of my room, take my computer and thrash it into pieces. It has happened several times with me that I wake up in the middle of the night and check if my desktop and laptop are all OK. I heaved a sigh of relief.

"Everything's OK man, just wake up," Rick said.

I got up, washed my face and sat on a chair to have some water.

"Yes, what is it?" I asked Rick.

"This guy was actually having a really bad time. He has written everything about her…" Rick answered.

"Aarav? I don't believe that. I saw them studying together in the campus gardens just last week." I said with doubt.

"Maybe. But if you go by what's written here, his relationship was far too complicated," said Rick, smiling.

"So you read the whole thing?" I asked this question because the time was 1 pm. It was lunch time, and it had been just a little over four hours since I went to sleep.

"Yeah. But Aarav was really bad at English. I wonder how he topped secondary school from ICSE board!" said Rick.

"He topped?" I was curious.

"Not only his school, he was also the state topper for ICSE," said Rick.

"Alright, now tell me the damn story man…" I was getting impatient.

"Sure. But after lunch…" said Rick.

Lunch was boring, as usual. We ate for mere sustaining ourselves. But I was more interested in listening to the story. I wanted to know what made such a brilliant guy commit suicide. I could understand committing suicide for getting bad grades and having a failed love affair at the same time. Such people need psychiatrists. But with good grades, suicide was a bad option even after having a failed love affair! There are so many girls out there in spite of the continuously dwindling sex ratio in India…why would someone chose to die for one specific girl, especially when he clearly has a bright future?

"Now let's begin," said Rick, "I shall narrate in first person, as Aarav," he declared.

"OK, cool with me." Did I even have another option?!

AARAV...

Hellllloooooo reader! I am your new host! I will take you through the rest of this journey, well, most of it. Sadly, Mr. Invisible won't be able to come with us. He's busy with Rick, trying to find out things – evidences, clues and what not – most of which I'm already aware of. You see, I know *everything*, and that is the reason why I chose to take you forward. So fasten your seatbelts folks, get yourself a cozy bed, couch, or anything that the bread-earners of your family could afford. If you're reading this on a train journey, especially in second class, just keep looking around after every couple of pages – someone might be in the lookout for your luggage. If you're even slightly like me, you won't be carrying anything more precious than a Chemistry text-book, but then, losing a text-book hurts like hell…

By the way, in the place where you are, they call me Aarav. Nice meeting you! Hope you're having a great time.

I know what you might be thinking. Let me clarify – I am not a bookworm, not the kind who nudges you all the time at school. I am just a simple guy, with simple ambitions.

I want to make it big.

Now let's come to the point. To make it big, the middle class student needs to study hard, and probably become an engineer or a doctor. I chose the former, because the latter spot was already taken up by Sunny bro, my elder brother.

Silly parents.

If one is a doctor, another shouldn't be. Not that I have a *deep interest* in Biology or anything, I'm just saying. Had bro taken up engineering, I would have been forced to study about 'Reproduction in Plants', Crap! Thanks Sunny bro, you made my life – better or worse, I don't know.

But wait, you just heard engineering right. You probably have friends who have made it to one of those great engineering colleges which churn out hordes of mindless good-for-nothing graduates. Surprisingly, most of them get into companies which pay them a hefty sum of money. If you're not one of them, it's absolutely nothing to worry about because your new friend Aarav is certainly one of them...

Yes, I'm one of those sleep-deprived, zealous, spineless *homo-sapiens*, who waste a lot of government money, to get themselves educated. No wonder, I don't actually want to become an engineer. All I want is to *make it big*, on a stage called 'Love' …

Yes, that's what I want to do. But I'm not sure how it will happen.

Yeah, I'm a dreamer. I dream about love. I dream about beautiful girls, with beautiful faces, but never see them. Have you ever dreamt of a beautiful girl and were able to remember her face? Never, right? Sad, but true...

But no worries dude! Unlike you, I'm very successful in love.

Just kidding. Just the *unlike* part, not the rest.

OK, so I used to have these amazingly enjoyable dreams, a few years ago.

I had this group of four guys, who craved for only two things in the world – Girls, girls, and girls.

Oh! Is that three? Sorry, I always get confused about girls. It is not only difficult, but impossible to understand them. If you're a girl, just accept it that you are a complicated piece of GOD's art! I know, I know, as a girl you think *'nobody understands me'* but, again, you will have to believe me when I say – *It's nobody's fault if they don't understand girls* – your species is made to be that way.

Seriously now, I will have to ask GOD to include a USER's MANUAL with every exotic piece of his art. I might have to do it right away.

But wait! You are waiting to listen to my story, right? Don't worry, it's a long story. Thanks for reading it until now. While I talk to GOD's secretary to get an appointment, I want you to do three things –

1. Leave this book aside, but don't forget the bookmark.
2. Get up, splash some water over your face and get refreshed.
3. Drink one full glass of water.

No…don't keep that glass aside without emptying it. *I am watching,* so be a loyal friend.

After you have done these three things, you are ready to move ahead. The road may be bumpy. And it is a non-stop journey.

Don't tell me I didn't ask you to ensure a cozy and comfortable position.

Ohh…*nature's call?* Don't worry, I'll allow you to answer it. Otherwise my appointment with GOD might get cancelled…

F4...

"*Haan* baby! I was missing you badly darling..." said Dhirendra over the phone. He had three things worth flaunting – a *filmi* surname viz. 'Kapur', a stack of hot girlfriends and one super-expensive mobile phone. He was tall, five-ten maybe, and wheat complexioned. I had met him just a few days ago and the way we got introduced to each other was too dramatic.

I was trying to call home and tell mom that I had reached safely, but there was some network problem with my phone. "Here, try calling from my phone," Dhirendra spoke, having observed me for a few minutes. My eyes immediately got fixed on his phone as he moved it towards me. That touchscreen device was tough to use. Touchscreens were new at that time. Somehow I managed to call mom but it got disconnected.

"So, what's up?" he asked me casually.

"Nothing..." I said, giving his phone back to him. It began to ring.

"Unknown number," he said and responded to the call,

"Yes darling! I was trying to call you baby…" he said without even listening to who it was on the call.

Suddenly he looked at me, and spoke, "I'm sorry. Yes, Aarav is here, just a second," and handed over the phone to me with a blank expression.

I became curious, and put the phone to my ear,

"Hello!"

It was mom's voice!

"Yes mom…yeah, it was my friend. Yes, he was talking with his friend…Yes mom, I'm fine…" I somehow managed the conversation and even she chose to skip it. Parents usually ignore a lot of things about their children in order to avoid embarrassing situations…

After the call, Dhirendra grinned…and that's how we became friends…

♡ ♡ ♡

"My aunt got these shoes for me from the USA. They cost $357," said Ronit. I was amazed. Avinash, however, wasn't much convinced. "C'mon, these aren't American shoes…" he began saying, "and what's the name of your aunt by the way?" he asked.

Ronit's face fell. We all called him 'Rony'. Ok just Bhalu called him 'Rony'. Alright, we called Avinash 'Bhalu'…no, just Rony called him 'Bhalu'…Aaarrrghhh!! Rony and Bhalu – Let's just call them by these names…

So, Rony had no answer to Bhalu's question. He got up, plugged in his earphones and was ready to leave the room.

"Now, where are you going with that weird music player from UK?" Bhalu mocked him. "Huh!" was all Rony could utter...

Rony had some unusual characteristics. He was brainless, fat, boastful, and mysteriously rich. He had blood relatives in nearly all parts of the world, at least that's what he used to tell us. To sum it all up, he was an incredibly small brain floating around in an incredibly large body. He had a fad for talking about himself. He could talk about himself for hours and hours and still not get tired. Bhalu was unusual too. He had not yet learnt how to use his brain. He could say anything to anyone. In the first week itself, he joined a movement to overhaul the mess system in order to improve the quality of food. When they were asked to meet the concerned highest authority in that regard, he went ahead and spoke straight in his face, "*Aap khana kha ke dekh lo ek baar*" (You come and have food once in the mess!)

♡ ♡ ♡

"I know a lot of people who call themselves 'DK', what's so cool in that?" Bhalu said, "I'll call him DKP!" he declared.

"Fucking hilarious! Yes, DKP it will be..." roared Rony while Dhirendra was busy texting on his phone. He didn't mind whatever we call him. So he was named DKP from that day onwards. It was a funny name.

But wait, what was I doing between these three dickheads?

I wasn't a freak, I didn't have a weird nickname and I wasn't rich either. I don't know. Although I didn't particularly like Rony, I somehow gelled well with these guys, and we together became F4 – Fabulous 4 – of the batch...

FLASHBACK... #1: How I met Tripti

It's strange how the mentality of people changes with age and time. At the age of fourteen, you love to fall in love. At the age of fifteen, you want to be loved. Change fifteen to fifty and you hate all those who even talk about love! Never mind the numbers, engineers really don't care about a few differences here and there. That is why I am fast-forwarding it a bit.

May 2008: I topped the state class tenth boards.

Awww…now don't be so jealous of me. I told you I am not like those who brag about it. Although in any given year, there will be only about 30-40 people like me in the country, I have the liberty to say that all of them are equally dumb. Not because I think they are…but because *I know* it.

So I began to be featured in the local newspaper, guiding other fellows to become as dumb as me, or even more, in the following year, I could see the bright smile on the face of my parents. It indicated that they saw the next *Albert Einstein* in me. Pretty close…if you ask me, I was pretty close to becoming Albert Einstein's laundryman's favourite *paan-wala*, had he been living at that time, that too in India and assuming he didn't do his own laundry. For that matter, in fact, I would have loved to be even that *paan-wala's* assistant…Believe me, being at the top of the state-board's merit list does mean top-of-the-world for parents who are over-obsessed with board exams. In reality, it meant that I was also roped into a rat-race that lay ahead …

FIVE HUNDRED DAYS LATER…

Now don't fuss over this. I have already told you I don't care much about numbers. Maybe it was indeed five hundred, or in the worst case give or take forty or fifty. The great engineering entrance exams were about to begin in about a fortnight. Well, you know my plight, don't you? I had to qualify these exams. Mom would usually say, 'This is the *only* thing we want from you.'

Are you serious Mom? Hahaha…This is just *one of the* 'only' things that you have ever wanted from me. It is with almost every other guy who takes up the divine task of qualifying engineering entrance exams. I am not saying I don't love my parents. Just that, at that age, everyone seems to be annoyed with their parents for some reason or the other. Some are annoyed because their parents simply crib at everything. If you're a girl of sixteen, the most dreaded thing would probably be to meet your mom in the middle of your college canteen while you are comfortably clinging on to the shoulders of that one awesome guy you want to give your whole life to. If you're that guy, you can still get away with it somehow.

One more specific reason why I clearly remember those days was Tripti. She was one year junior to me, and she was the solution to all my problems, at least temporarily.

When we entered class twelfth, most of the guys used to get their journals and practical books completed by juniors, i.e. students from class eleventh. Now I wasn't one of those selfish, bully seniors. I didn't want to burden the juniors in any way. But at that same time I couldn't risk doing all that boring stuff all by myself. In the end I decided I shall write as much as I could, and leave out the rest. So, one fine day I began with the Physics practical. I sat down in one lonely chair at one corner of the canteen and began writing. It was lunch time. Almost all tables were occupied. The corner ones were usually the least preferred tables. After a while, a girl came near my table. I was too busy to notice who she was, but I could say it was a girl from the jasmine perfume she had put on. She put her bag on the table and said, "I hope you don't mind if I take this seat…"

As I said, I was too much engrossed to even notice her so I nodded casually, indicating that I didn't mind… She put her remaining books on the table and sat on the chair opposite to mine. She had ordered noodles which were served almost immediately.

"Did you have lunch?" she asked me. I didn't listen. She spoke again, "You're too busy it seems. What are you doing?"

She picked up my physics textbook and began to read, "Practicals??"

Now that was enough to break my attention. I stopped writing. Keeping my pen away I looked at her with both awe and confusion. She smiled. I got lost.

In the usual uniform, the red tie complemented well with her red lips. Her hairs weren't tied up, and it made her fair face glow more prominently. Her glasses complemented so well with her face that I immediately got attracted to that look. She blinked her eyes innocently and with that I lost whatever part of my attention was still remaining with those physics practicals.

"Hullo...!! I am Tripti by the way," she spoke confidently. I realized I had been staring at her for the past few seconds continuously. I broke eye contact. A glass of water was placed near her. I didn't even ask her before taking it and gulping down all the water it had. She was slightly amazed. Now I decided to answer her questions one by one.

"Yes, that's physics. I'm trying to complete all this by weekend. Hope it gets done," I said.

"Ohh... I thought you were from my class. But you turned out to be my senior!" she sounded a bit excited and frightened at the same time.

"Umm...yeah, but you see all my classmates get these things done by juniors. And I hate that. So I decided to do it myself, whatever I could," I explained her. She asked me again about lunch. I ordered fried rice on her insistence. And then we began to talk. And I began to check her out.

"So, umm...why do you hate the idea of asking your juniors to do it?" she asked casually. She could talk sensibly, a rare quality among girls.

"It's just...I don't want to burden anyone. And...we all

should do our own work I guess," I answered as genuinely as I could.

"Well that's great. No senior has asked me yet to do any work. Who knows, someone might, soon," she said as she moved her fork randomly over the noodles showing slight disinterest towards it.

"Who knows, yes," I didn't really know how to answer this.

"Well, don't you find it boring? This work…" she sounded concerned.

"Boring? To the core! But I've decided to not push myself. I'll do only as much as I can," I replied.

She looked worried for a while, but then her face brightened.

"How about some help? I'm getting bored anyway," she said cheerily.

I hadn't expected she would offer help. I did want some help of course, but not from her. Or maybe, on second thoughts, yes, I would love if she could help me. She seemed to be a nice girl. Moreover, she seemed to be genuinely concerned.

"I don't know…I mean, I don't know if I want you to help me out," I said as I picked up my pen to continue writing.

"Ohh c'mon! Give me that!" she said as she pulled my notebook towards her. "I'll manage this, don't worry," she reassured me with her infectiously cute smile. I smiled too. And indeed, the problem did get solved!

After lunch, we discussed about the part she required to complete and I clarified any doubts she had.

"Here, take my phone number. Give me a missed call so I can know yours. Will help us keep in touch," she said, very casually.

"Yeah. OK. Here…" I took my cellphone and called up on her number. I saved her number. She saved my number and smiled. I smiled too. Problem solved, or created? I don't know…Her jasmine perfume lingered on me for a long time after she left.

FLASHFRONT... #1: How I met Nivedita

August 2010

"Excuse me. I need to go to the bank. Can you please tell me where is the bank?" asked a girl in a pink top. She was searching for the bank. Of course, that was clearly evident from her words. The guard was clueless. Maybe he was new too. Now IIT was one large campus overstuffed with amenities but devoid of signboards. Some felt it wasn't necessary, some felt it was, and others simply cared a fuck about it! One may be tempted to open up a debate on this, but seniors would simply outwit anyone with this one simple sentence – 'Do you have signboards inside your home?'

New students used to face problems finding directions, and I was one of them too. I didn't know where the bank was. In fact it had been just a week since I had been on this campus and still I always had to ask someone the way if I wanted to get back to my hostel without much fuss. But that day I simply couldn't control the urge to walk in the situation and help her out.

"Hey! Come, I'll take you to the bank," I smiled and offered guiding her to the bank.

She looked at me, and then looked at the guard.

"Alright, let's go…"

Now the real problem arises. Where is this fucking bank?

"I'm Aarav by the way," I began to speak, nervously.

"Hi! I'm Nivedita. Just joined. This is a very difficult place for new people…"

"Yeah, but you'll get used to it. I joined just a week ago and now it's not all that confusing," I said as I scanned all around me to find someone who could tell me where the bank was.

"Are you sure it's this way, coz the guard there was pointing me the other way," she asked.

"No…I mean, yes, but this one's a shortcut. You wouldn't want to go the long way, would you?"

She nodded. Just then I spotted DKP. He was busy with his cellphone.

"DK…P…" I called him. He, at once, looked in my direction. I instructed him to come to me.

"Just wait here for a moment, I'll be back," I told Nivedita as I and DKP moved to a safe distance from where she couldn't hear us.

"Dude, where is the bank?" I asked him, whispering slightly.

"Why?"

I gave him a darned look.

"Ok…take the right after this, and head straight towards the new cafeteria. You know the new cafeteria, dude?"

I nodded.

"Ok…so, just behind the new cafeteria. That's your bank…"

I thanked him profusely for this.

"By the way, that chick is hot. What's her name?"

"Nivedita. She has just joined. I might even take her on some kind of private campus tour soon!"

And we both exchanged villainous glances, like the one's college boys usually do when they talk about hot girls and porn.

Luckily then, I could take her to the bank. She thanked me.

"Which branch by the way?"

"Computer Science," she said.

"Oh! Well, then see you in class…"

She smiled. I smiled too. Problem solved, or created? I don't know…

♡ ♡ ♡

"Dude, he met some girl today and now this is the result," DKP told Rony.

I had rejected their idea to go for a movie in the evening. "Man, are you mad? It's just been a week into this college and you're behaving like *Devdas*…" said Bhalu. After a lot of anticipation, I broke my silence –

"I can't do anything right now…because right now, I can

just think of a blue-eyed *apsara*…"

My words immediately got Rony interested. He pulled out his earphones and began listening.

"She is my dream girl. She is one of her kind. Ooohh, she has the right mix of beauty and oomph! If beauty with brains is rare, I'm sure she has none of the latter! I wonder how she even got into this university. Maybe GOD had sent her for me…"

Silence.

"I feel like shouting out her name. What a beautiful name. I just love her name. I love everything about her. Her single dimpled smile has made me her immediate admirer, and secret lover. What will happen if I will begin seeing her smile daily? I don't know how long I'll be able to hide this…"

Silence.

"Her name is…Nivedita… Ms. Nivedita Raj…"

Silence.

Now this was the limit. Rony began to smile which slowly turned into an ugly laughter. Bhalu began to laugh too. DKP was too busy in his phone. Fucking retards, all of them! Anyway, so that evening I didn't join them for the movie…

FLASHBACK... #2: Life with Tripti

October 2009

That evening she texted me.

Heyyy! R U Busy? 😊 *–Tripti*

People like me can be ever-busy and ever-available at the same time. So of course, I was not busy that evening. Actually, she wanted me to accompany her to the bookstore.

"Bookstores are boring," I said as she began browsing through books and handing the selected ones over to me. She just smiled and picked another book from the 'New Releases' section. I was already holding a heap of seven books in my hands and she added another one on top of it.

"And listen, give some books to me..." she sounded genuinely concerned, as she usually does.

"No no no... It's absolutely OK..." I said, nodding my head. She looked pretty browsing books, but then another section of the bookstore was much more interesting for me – the Adult section.

As soon as I saw *Maxim*, *FHM*, and the likes tucked in one place, all my attention got concentrated on that very place. Covers with semi-nude girls made my body temperature rise by at least half a degree. You must've seen those magazines showing sensuously covered assets of girls with gorgeous figures in the side-view, right? It's simply amazing. And amazing it was, when my eyes, brain and body stopped moving, in response to the huge collection of magazines that lay there. Slowly but steadily, I was automatically being pulled closer to that teenage treasure. Within moments, I would hold one of them in my hands, and touch the preciously printed pages showing carefully crafted beauties with glowing skin and deep eyes. I was now standing in front of the block, which had several shelves. My hand began to slowly move towards any randomly reachable attractive pleasure-giving sheets of printed paper compiled in an easily readable format…

Just when I was about to touch those heavenly assets on the cover of *FHM*, I heard a voice coming from behind. As I said, my eyes, brain and body had stopped moving, and they were being controlled by some other stimulus. This voice suddenly put an end to that stimulus.

"Are you sure you can carry those books…"

Before I could look behind, the seven, sorry, eight books which I was carrying, all fell on the floor. She immediately ran towards me. But before situations could get any worse, I came back to my senses and sat down to pick up the fallen books. Co-incidentally, her hands went straight towards the book which I had put my hands on, just a few nanoseconds back.

That touch made my heart skip a beat. She withdrew her hand and let me pick up that book. Wow! That was something which usually happens in movies…

So in this way I helped her with books, she helped me with my studies. It seemed perfect but only until I discovered her in dreamland that night…

From the next day onwards, we made it a point to have lunch together in school. And because of her, I began attending school more often. In fact, everyday! Except Saturdays and Sundays, of course, but then you get it right?

♡ ♡ ♡

"So don't you have any friends?" I enquired. We sat in the school canteen, at the same old corner table where we had first met

"Umm…let's see. There's Saumya, Divyansh…and how can I forget Vatan…" she giggled.

GOD! Tell me Saumya is a girl!

"And what about Swati?"

"She's a dahling! She's my bestest friend!"

I grinned. Yes, girls have this very peculiar way of talking about their best friends. If you talk like that about your male best friend, he'd say, "Dude, for God's sake, I'm not GAY!"

"Yeah, but you know, most of the times I am thinking about you and your work these days so…I think I haven't met anyone in two weeks," she laughed at her own confession.

She keeps thinking about me and me my work? Wait, Me AND my work?

Me OR my work?

Why not just ME?

"Umm, by the way, I think we're done with your practicals and stuff, right! It's time to celebrate!"

Whoa! She was being too nice now.

"Yes, of course," I said, trying not to look too excited.

We celebrated by having dinner together that evening, in a romantic restaurant close to the school. I had to spend all my savings to make sure she could order all that she wanted. But then it was really worth it.

♥ ♥ ♥

"Hey, I found a DVD in one of your books, the physics one I guess…" she informed me over the phone.

"What DVD?"

"Nothing's written on it, just a small 'X', and nothing else…"

Now that's when you regret keeping porn DVDs in your books. Well, no matter how cool you are with a girl, the last thing you would want to share with her is porn.

"Ok, I got it. You can give it back to me tomorrow…"

"Umm…Okies! But is it a movie? Is it X-Men?" she asked excitedly.

No. It's not X-Men. It's XXX-Women.

"No it's…I mean…it's…" I fumbled. I was thinking hard to frame something.

"It's actually a virus-infected DVD. X for Danger, got it?"

"Oohh..." she got a bit frightened.

"Now whatever happens, don't open that DVD on your computer. Better don't run it on your DVD player too...it can infect just about anything..." I said dramatically.

I heard the sound of some books falling on the floor.

"You OK?" I asked.

"Yeah, I'm fine. I'll give it back to you tomorrow..."

Problem averted...

As the entrance exams came closer, I needed to study for a longer time than usual. This meant not meeting Tripti at other times of the day, though we still used to have lunch together at school. We liked each other, and that was pretty much clear. I was either too busy or too shy to tell her that I loved her. Meanwhile, Tripti was expecting me to confess my love for her.

"If he's taking so much time, why don't you tell him about your feelings?" Swati suggested.

"I don't know...I thought it's a guy's thing..."

"It's alright; he's busy with exams and stuff. So you must understand him no Tripti..."

"Ok...I'll propose to him tomorrow, if he doesn't. It's his birthday; He has called me home..."

"That'll be good Tripti baby! All the best!"

FLASHFRONT... #2: The Sri Lankan NRI

Time flew by, slowly but steadily. But time is too treacherous, believe me. Since Nivedita was hot, she became an instant celebrity on the campus. And one fine day...

2nd September 2010, 8 pm

She broke my heart into a million pieces, and now every piece loves her in a million ways.

I just had a heart-breaking moment. It feels bad. I asked her out, it was a sort of date. I didn't know she was such a good player. I knew she had a soft corner for Aniket, aka 'Akki', that Sri Lankan guy at the university, but never knew she had slept with him already. Okay, I exaggerated on the last sentence. But the fact remains, they are an item!

Maybe his NRI status attracted her. Or maybe his smile. I've heard he has a cute smile. Wow...these days anyone can have a cute smile. But my question is – why did she go out with me?

"She just wanted free dinner dude," said Rony.

What he was saying is true. We just went to that damn hotel, had dinner while talking about the university, and came back without changing the topic. She might have sent a few hundred SMSes within those hundred and fifty minutes that we were together, and she would smile regularly in between them. My innocent brain just couldn't make it out. If rumours are to be believed, she had been walking hand in hand with that NRI a few days ago in the campus. Some of my hostel-mates report that he even plucked some flowers from the gardens and gifted her, after which they went out in his car...

In his car? Damn! He has a car?!!

Rich, spoilt, NRI...

These are the qualities that attract women towards any person. I don't care - I'm just feeling low, very low.

I spent the whole night thinking about Nived, and that Sri Lankan. Anyway, I don't want to go down as a loser this time. That is the reason why, even though I know Nived would go for that Sri Lankan, considering he has all the time and wealth in the world, I would still go to the extent of proposing my love to her. I am quite sure she would turn me down, but what's wrong in trying? Eleven lakh students give that damn engineering entrance exam every year and only about eleven thousand students go to places which are meaningful. So that's about one in a hundred. Isn't that called taking chance? Imagine you need to cross a large river with another hundred people, and you know that just one of these would not drown. What would you do?

If you're one of those peculiar guys who instantly identified yourself with me, you might be wondering how I suddenly became so good with numbers! See, love makes you smart.

In the morning, while roaming in the hostel, I sent her a text message:

Canteen, 1:30 sharp, hot paranthas?

A quick reply followed:

Sure...

Just then, Rony and Bhalu came back from their regular morning jogging sessions. It was already 10 am. I wonder if they actually wake up at five, because if that's true, they must have run at least 20 kilometers by now.

"I just love Selena Gomez," said Bhalu, "Can I, by any chance, get to marry her?"

"Only in your dreams!" cried Rony.

"Man, she's just my age. I'm sure I can knock off Bieber – he's not a man anyway," Bhalu tried to justify.

I could sense that the mere thought of Selena was making the guy lose patience. I felt I should help the guy out, and so I said calmly,

"See you just need to do a few simple things – become awesomely rich, then kill bieber and put him off somewhere, and then get a plastic surgeon to make you look exactly like him. That's it! Believe me, it's the single best method to get hooked up with Selena..."

"And then of course, he needs to learn English…" exclaimed Rony, "and dude, you can take kissing lessons from me," he said turning to Bhalu.

"Buzz off Rony," Bhalu moved towards his room.

I wonder if it's worth doing all that for a girl like Selena. Well, I just want Nived.

I didn't have lunch, as I was immersed in her exotic thoughts. I was waiting impatiently for the clock to strike one. When it did, I put on my favorite white shirt with a brilliant blue denim jacket, and jeans. Spraying some *AXE* and applying Set wet, I filled up my chest and tried to look like a stud. With every notch and corner of my body beaming with confidence, I was ready to jump into Nived's ocean of love. I just hope that ocean doesn't have Sri Lankan piranhas!

I reached the canteen exactly at 1 pm. The next thirty minutes were the longest thirty minutes of my life. Those minutes made me so vulnerable that I could actually kiss Akki's crap if he let go of Nived. I could just do anything to make Nivedita accept my love for her. With crossed fingers, I continued to wait, my eyes fixed on the path which originated from the Girls' Hostel…

At exactly forty minutes past one, almost ten minutes late, that ever-graceful angelic figure of Nivedita appeared. My heart skipped a beat as I began feeling nervous about the whole situation. She was wearing a sleeveless pink top with a denim skirt. She was definitely the kind of girl every guy would dream about, although I would certainly not like that. But she was amazing.

Our eyes met, and made me feel all the more nervous. She had applied eyeliner or maybe it was *kajal*. Whatever it was, it made her eyes look magically attractive. 'Would I be able to tell her how I felt?' this seemed to be like the question of the decade. As she came closer to me, I smiled involuntarily. Her ruby red colored lips parted seductively so as to reveal her sparkling teeth which made me feel the urge to kiss her beautiful, tender lips. I moved closer to her as she said, "Hi!"

"You look like an angel," I blurted out. Her face brightened up and soon faded to end into a cute blush. I took it as a positive indication, although I knew I was just consoling myself. But I didn't care as long as it made me happy. The smile on my face was fixed.

"Thanks..." her majestic voice sounded like that of a magical fairy, "Let's go sit in the garden," she suggested sweetly.

We sat facing the small lake which had several peacocks drinking from it. Some birds were flying about the area; squirrels were running around the place, making the environment feel heavenly. I suddenly realized we had skipped the whole idea of *paranthas*. For a moment I felt she did that knowingly. Suddenly I realized she had picked up a rose from a nearby bush, and was plucking out its petals one by one.

Man! This was pure Bollywood style love!

With every odd petal her face would brighten, and fade away with every even petal. For each even petal that she plucked, she would nod anxiously and then pluck out another petal, close her eyes and smile as if she was in someone's arms and she was enjoying that pleasurable moment. As I was watching her do this, something was going on in my mind – "She loves me, she loves me not…she loves me, she loves me not…she loves me…….."

Suddenly I heard someone's name being called in a sweet voice. This voice was very familiar to me. It was the same voice which mesmerized my senses day in and day out. It was the same voice that filled up all my dreams. It is the same voice that kept echoing in my ears all the time.

But the name? The name was familiar too. It was the name of a person I was not very fond of. It was the name of a person I constantly felt jealous of. It was the name of a person who had all the three qualities needed to woo a girl – rich, spoilt, NRI.

Yes, it was that very name…

"Ohh, Aniket…" Nivedita was moaning seductively, sometimes kissing the unworthy flower which was just martyred to signify her emotions or anxiety or both, and sometimes rubbing it over her smooth pinkish tinged cheek. "Mmmm…" she was lost in her dreamland, with Akki and I could only see this from a distance.

My senses turned numb. A large ocean of grief was about to pour from my eyes in the form of tears. *Rony was right*, I thought. Without a word, I got up from the bench. I picked up a small stone from the ground and threw it as hard as I could. It landed right in the middle of the lake. Nivedita got distracted by the sound and turned her head upwards to look at me. I gave her a short glance, hastily turned and ran as fast as I could.

"Aarav, where are you going, we need to have lunch….. Remember………." she called to me, but her last words faded and I couldn't hear them. I continued to run towards my hostel, with tears flowing uncontrollably from my eyes. I just didn't care about the world at this moment.

I had failed again, once again…

FLASHBACK... #3: Heartbreak

28th January 2010

So it was my birthday and I had invited her, just her to my home. I had several things in mind – a sweet proposal, sweet chocolates, and a sweet day.

To begin with, let me tell you that it would be irresponsible on my part if I wouldn't inform you that my seventeenth birthday was a complete disaster and turned out to be the most hurtful day of my life. Nothing went on as expected. I wanted to do something that could leave a deep impression upon her heart. I was novice about all this back then.

Here's what I had decided to say, "Which chocolate do you like more – Dairy Milk or Five Star? Since it's a special day for me, I want to make it special for you too. The time I have spent with you in the last several months was the best time of my life. Your voice is so sweet; I can keep listening to you all through my life. I love your sense of humor. Let's take our friendship to the next level…" While ending my love confession I would present her with her favorite chocolate, with both Five Star and Dairy Milk in either of my pockets.

And then I would continue, "Today, I make you the queen of my heart…"

That was the sweetest proposal I could think of. You see, studying for entrance exams takes a toll on your romantic capabilities. I had to get ready. She was supposed to arrive by 5 pm.

All my preparations on one side, and what actually happened on the other side…It was an unbearable shock for me. To start with, my mom got really sick. She had an unbearable pain in her left knee. She couldn't even walk properly, but somehow cooked food. As the pain became terrible around 3:00, she began to weep and shout. I decided that today was not the right time to talk to my dream girl, let alone celebrate my birthday. I had mixed feelings, but I decided to give it my best shot today and propose to her. But things grew worse when Malini aunty and Rutuj bhai came to see mom. She had to come down and finally my room was occupied by two aliens and my mom. So practically now there was no place to talk to her. I was waiting for her to show up, with lot of confusions in my mind. But things turned out to be too ugly, as she didn't show up even by 7 in the evening.

I called up Swati, who didn't receive my call for the first four times. When she did receive, her words were as painful as a thousand knives stabbing all over my body –

"Trip…tripti…is no more…"

I was stunned.

This page left blank in the memory of Tripti...

BACK TO PRESENT: Kaavya…

3rd September 2010

I spent the rest of the day in complete disconnection from the rest of the world around me. I had switched off my phone as I was not in the mood to talk to anyone. I couldn't throw Nivedita out of my mind for quite some time. The fact that we had dinner together once and that she would come with me for walks, was something that would always remain with me.

How could she be so mean? I thought. Maybe she considered me just a friend and nothing more than that. It wasn't her fault, to be fair. But then, everything is fair in love and war, so it wouldn't be wrong if I said that what she did to me was unfair.

In the evening, I didn't even feel like having dinner. Bhalu coaxed me into having at least a bit of rice. As I sat at the dining table in the mess, the food looked irritating. I turned my head around the mess to see different sorts of people. Some fatsos were busy stuffing anything that they found on the plate (or around it) into their mouths. Their pot-bellies confirmed that they had been doing that for ages. Some guys, like Umang, had two *rotis* on their plates while they ate only one on any given occasion. Umang, though, was rare. He ate just *half* a *roti*. Others around him were rather engrossed in discussing about *maal* and non-*maal* categories of girls on the campus. Had there been a B. Tech course in 'Deciphering Girls' they would have definitely got themselves enrolled. Seriously!

Rony, one of such fatsos, was furiously gobbling up all the salad and rice. He had bought a *Kurkure* pack, and was using it in place of pickles.

I picked up the spoon on my plate and tried to mix some rice with *dal* to make up a mouthful. Then I tried to force myself to have some of it. As the morsel approached my mouth, I felt an intense desire to throw it away. For a moment, my hands stopped as the spoon touched my lips. The next moment I found that the spoon was no more in my hand but lying under the dining table in front of me as I had thrown it fiercely, something that caught the attention of almost everyone in the mess. I tried to avoid eye-contact with any of the people, hurriedly drank some water and rushed out of the mess. I was feeling so irritated, I even puked out the water that was in my mouth. I just wanted to stay away from everything.

"Seriously, I think you should allow us to help you out man," said a voice from behind. It was DKP.

"Please leave me alone," I spoke, trying to control myself.

"Maybe we could go to the canteen and have some ice-cream or something you like," Rony said.

I told you he is an asshole. Even after stuffing about a dozen *rotis*, he still has room for ice-cream and stuff.

"You'll definitely feel better, even Kaavya's coming…" DKP tried to convince me.

I gave him a suspicious look. What had Kaavya got to do with all this? Anyway, the sound of her name relieved me of my stress to some extent. I felt a new kind of enthusiasm. Suddenly I wanted to go to the canteen.

Kaavya? Yes…I haven't yet told you about her. She happened sometime back, when I was still under the influences of Nivedita…DKP had suggested her name to me, and it happened like this…

♡ ♡ ♡

23rd August 2010, 10:15 am

The classroom was all full, except the last row. That row is always empty. I don't understand how some guys manage to skip all the lectures. The electronics professor was trying to explain something about semi-conductors. But I was interested in finding a mirror which can reflect my intense beam of *LOVE*. My eyes are emitting strong radiations of *LOVE* in all directions. I was just hoping that somebody receives them and we begin to communicate…

But my special focus is on Kaavya today. She is wearing a cute, pink top and tight blue jeans. She has the most perfect curves, just the perfect height. Her smile is as beautiful as that of an angel. The way she carries herself is amazing. I am observing her movements for the last class and she is quite impressive. She carries herself gracefully, and I can't help staring at her from the corner of the third row. She is seated in the first row. How come girls always sit in the first row? Well, maybe they know what guys like me do all the time in class; something that would be impossible if they were to sit in the last row. My eyes shift regularly from checking out Nivedita to sneak a bit into Kaavya. I was lost in dreamland, with Nivedita slowly caressing my hair while I lay in her lap, when suddenly a shrill voice called out.

"47..."

The mathematics professor turned up her head to throw up an I-know-you-guys-are-dull look at the class and called again,

"Roll No. 47? Miss Kaavya Joshi..."

There was a sudden silence in the class. I was still in a fixed position when my eyes suddenly met those of Kaavya. For a moment, all my cerebral activity stopped. I was unsure of what was going on there. Was she sneaking into my dreams? I became more alert and opened my eyes wide, shifted from a relaxed position to an attentive one and found that while I was checking out Nivedita in dreamland, Kaavya was checking me out right in the middle of the class when the attendance was being called out. The whole class was checking both of us out in turn. Kaavya hurriedly turned towards the old freaked out professor,

"Yes ma'am!" she sighed.

The professor waved her head in dismay and registered her presence.

"Please try to be attentive next time," said the lady who held a doctorate in mathematics but didn't even pass high school in the most important subject of life – LOVE. *She was single.*

And talking of being single, I wonder if she would come on a date with me…just once…

"She is freaking 42 years old!" exclaimed Bhalu, who was sitting next to me. I gave him an I-am-shocked look.

I hope he was not reading my mind, and I hope you are not my professor. By the way, isn't 42 the answer of life, universe and everything? Shouldn't it be 47 instead? Umm… Just asking…

♡ ♡ ♡

Back to the present times, I had no choice but to agree to the decision of my friends.

"Ok…let's go," I told DKP in a feeble voice.

"Wuhoo! Love is in the air!" Bhalu hooted. I sort of blushed. I don't know what it was supposed to mean, and I could not explain how I was feeling at that moment. But I really felt the urge to see Kaavya and talk to her now. I just wanted to get over with the whole Nived-*wala* episode.

"But the fact is that DKP is throwing a party, for his darling Suchi," commented Rony, "In that case, all of us wouldn't mind giving company, what say guys?" he grinned. Everyone nodded.

At 9:30 pm, four of us – I, DKP, Rony and Bhalu – set out for the canteen. DKP was trying his level best to keep me cheered up. He was aware of the Nivedita episode and wanted to help me come of it. He was really behaving like a big brother. While I was fighting an already lost war with Nivedita, he got hooked up with Suchita. In a way, that left me with just Kaavya as an option. With Suchi gone after my closest friend, I had to bury all feelings for her before they became strong enough to topple over our friendship. But that is another story altogether…

The eight minute long walk to the canteen was by far the most enriching walk in the campus. The whole path was bordered by beautiful flowers, shrubs and bushes. Even in the darkness of the night, one could smell them and say that they were some rare species of fragrant roses. This made the way to canteen all the more romantic. It had been rumored that anyone walking on this path almost always thought about his dream girl at least once.

We were about twelve meters away from the canteen when I could see Suchi and Kaavya waiting for us. They must not have anticipated that there would be the other two idiots with us. But wait, who was Kaavya expecting with DKP? Was it all planned? Was she just accompanying Suchi or was it about something else…Girls are mysterious, in the first place.

"Hieee!" exclaimed Suchi looking at DKP. They exchanged naughty glances. I turned my eyes towards Kaavya who was standing away from the rest of us shyly.

"Hi," I said softly, looking at Kaavya from a distance. She smiled.

"Kaavya, maybe we want to have ice-creams," started Rony.

"Sure!" she turned towards Rony and they began walking towards the canteen counter.

"Ok, so what do we have here, umm…Caramel, Vanilla…" said Rony as he skimmed through the menu of ice-creams and desserts, "Which one would you like to have?" he asked Kaavya.

"Why don't we buy a large ice-cream sundae and share a few spoonfuls?" Kaavya suggested.

"I don't think so…how about one large ice-cream sundae for me, and two large cones for you couples…and of course, Bhalu can have a spoonful or two from mine," suggested Rony.

Kaavya gave her a dry look. 'What does he mean by two couples,' she might have thought. I was watching this drama, when she looked at me. Her face suddenly brightened up, and a fresh smile appeared.

"Rony, I think that would be perfect," said she as they placed an order for one large ice-cream sundae (with two spoons), one large ice-cream cone with chocolate flavor for Suchi-DKP and another one with Vanilla flavor for Kaavya (and possibly me!).

After a couple of minutes, they returned with three ice-creams. Kaavya handed one cone to Suchi. Rony gladly went away with his large sundae to feed his monstrous belly. Kaavya came close to me, and handed over the vanilla cone to me.

As I took the cone from her, I glanced at her from head to toe. She was one beautiful artwork crafted to perfection. Not an inch of fat here or there, and probably the most exciting curves just in the right places. The skin-tight pink top went well with her bluish grey capris, making her look sensuous. I was observing the complicated patterns that appeared just below her belly button where her top overlapped the belt loops of her jeans, and just couldn't take my eyes off it, when suddenly I felt someone grabbing my hand softly. The feeling was so exciting, that it suddenly made me take a sharp breath while a wave of sensation passed all over my body. When I looked up, Kaavya was licking the ice-cream cone while it was still in my hand, which was in her hand now.

"Mmm…I'm hungry you see…" she explained, as her face burst into a cute smile. She probably had the cutest smile I had ever seen.

"Hmm…you have it too," she moved the cone closer to my mouth as if hinting that I could indeed have a bite while she held it in her beautiful hands.

Now in such a situation, believe me, you shouldn't feel too shy or alert. Nobody will kill you if you simply move forward, hold the girl's hand, and take a large bite from the ice-cream. If you're able to hold her hand even after you've taken a bite, then it explains you are one step closer…one step closer to either having her for your girlfriend, or being hit by her sandals.

In my case, however, I was too shy to be even able to let her hold my hand for long. "I….I don't …fe..feeel like having any," I coughed out the words nervously.

"C'mon Aarav, what's the matter with you?" asked Bhalu. He was probably left out of the group for two reasons – he didn't have a girl, and he didn't get any ice-cream.

Immediately I realized that Kaavya indeed liked me, but I couldn't reciprocate her feelings there. To change the topic, I turned towards Rony,

"You fatso, *saale bhukkad*...couldn't share your large ice-cream with Bhalu," I screamed at Rony who was engrossed in slurping the whole container of the sundae, with some ice-cream on his nose, right cheek and near his chin.

"That's disgusting!" Kaavya cried.

I turned towards her, and then looked at my watch. It was twenty minutes past ten. The girls needed to be back at the girl's hostel by half past ten. She would go in a couple of minutes. I didn't want to be a complete failure – *thrice!*

"Hey leave that fatso, read this."

I opened a special folder on my phone which contained some romantic and funny messages, and began showing her...

One boy went 2 meet his gf, whn he came back home mom asked
'kahan gaye the?'
Boy: us se milne
Mom: kis liye?
Boy: haan bahut kiss liye :D

She burst into laughter. This was just what I wanted. After reading a few more messages, she took my phone in her hand and began reading more...

"Can I forward this one to myself, please?" she asked cutely.

I wanted to tell her that she could probably forward anything from me to herself without my permission, but I was too shy, and I just said, "Yeah, sure!"

I would anyway get her mobile number.

She forwarded a few messages from my phone, probably three or four, after which no more messages got sent. Now it was time for the girls to leave. DKP and Suchi had some eye-to-eye conversation as they walked out of the canteen, probably experiencing that immense pleasure which came from looking into your lover's eyes, and brushing your shoulder against theirs while walking. I know it, because I have had these and many more pleasures, innumerable times… in dreamland.

Kaavya returned my phone and said, "I'll send the other messages later. They're so nice."

She was still smiling in a way that made me lose consciousness.

Her impressive ways had left me day-dreaming about her, and I didn't realize when the girls were gone. We sat near the canteen for another half an hour. I mentally noted that I need to do a few things…

1. Get my phone recharged with a message pack tariff

2. Practice saying 'I love you' in front of the mirror

3. Get some new funky apparel

NUMBER THEORY...

3rd September 2010, 11:15 pm

"Yellow is your favorite color," began Rony, "and you loved a girl before coming here but couldn't get her." I was amazed. Rony seems to be a hell of a palm-reader.

"Tell me more about my lines. Where will they take me?" I demanded.

"You will go far. Very far. But you need to keep your numbers in order," said Rony, a little seriously.

"Numbers? As in...?"

"11 will be good for you, while 6 will be unimaginably bad. Try to avoid all occurrences of the number 6 in your life. For a two or more digit number, add all the digits and try to avoid it if the result is 6. 11 will show you the path to *nirvana,* that is, salvation," Rony ended the speech with a smile. I couldn't believe he understood numerology. Either I am too dumb or he is my savior. By the way, I had a strong urge to ask him, "Dude, what about the other numbers? Am I concerned with only 11 and 6?" Of course, every number was either good for me, or bad for me. So, there must be some categorization, right. Like, you know, '7 is great for you if you are dating a blonde on weekends' or '3 is bad for you if you are playing water football against a hippopotamus'. Huh?! Give me a break! What has the number got to do with dating? Playing football against a hippo is bad on any day, on any planet, and I'm sure – for any number!

Rony's words now echoed in my ears.

'11 will be good for you, while 6 will be unimaginably bad. Try to avoid all occurrences of the number 6 in your life.'

Nivedita's birthday was on 6th June.

Kaavya was roll number 47, that makes it 11. Her birthday comes on 11th November, which is same as two elevens. 'Was this all a coincidence or a sign from GOD himself?' I was unable to understand the reasons. Her interest in me was very obvious.

I thought Rony was right and maybe even Saturdays were bad for me. I thought Nivedita was never meant for me.

I thought I shouldn't have got attracted to her in the first place.

Suddenly, Nivedita's figure didn't seem all that hot. Her smile wasn't really magical. Her lips weren't that tender after all. Love numbs your senses. It makes you like everything about the person you love. Once the influence of love wears out, your real thoughts resurface. I was glad that she was hooked up with a Sri Lankan and not an American. NRI didn't mean an Indian guy staying in a third world country would be considered rich. Aaah! Now don't try to explain to me that Sri Lanka isn't one. I already told you I am not great with facts! You get the message, don't you? Of course, you are my friend; you have some duties and responsibilities towards me. So just forget everything else and continue reading...

KAAVYA...

Next day was a Sunday. I mean, it is still a Sunday. 19th September 2010 would always be a Sunday no matter which country you belong to.

As usual, we were trying to zero down on a movie we could watch on a Sunday morning. Rony was behaving oddly. He was completely bowled over by a girl named Esha Mathur, who was in the third year. So much so that he had been collecting all her Facebook photos since morning and even went to the extent of saying something extravagantly hilarious to Bhalu. Here's how it went,

"Man! Esha Mathur is unbelievably hot! If I am granted one special wish from GOD, I would ask him to give me Eshaaa.... I curse the time I was born dude...I should've either born three years earlier, or else never even born..."

Probably, his parents wouldn't approve of him marrying an older girl. Or maybe it wasn't about his parents. Maybe he disliked the idea of being in a relationship with an older girl himself. Whatever the reason, he was really furious about the fact that he couldn't *patao* that specific hot girl, who had another hundred people drooling around her.

My cause of concern was, however, something far more severe. I wanted to go out with Kaavya. I wanted to talk to her privately, get to know more about her, find out if she was like me, or if we could get hooked up or something. But it wasn't so simple for me. I had had just one meeting with her and I wasn't sure...I wasn't sure if I could ask her to go out, irrespective of whether she actually wanted to go out with me or not. Another issue was that it was a Sunday and, if not today, I'd have to wait for another week to take her out. Nooo....you're getting me wrong again! I didn't study on weekdays! But the fact is girls studied a lot, and they needed to study even on Sundays. So any girl would get pretty pissed off, if I asked her to keep aside her books and come on a date with me. It could've worked if I was among the likes of Robert Pattinson, which would require an expensive plastic surgery, but never – as I actually was...

But then that Sunday came and went...like any other Sunday. The next target was a week later, another Sunday...

FIVE DAYS LATER, Friday, 24th September 2010, 10 pm

Hmm...another weekend ahead. I had done enough exercise in the last five days to be able to ask her out. We had been exchanging messages at the rate of four-five messages a day. I was supposed to increase this number a hundred times, as per Rony. But I was fine with it as of now. Earlier this week, on Wednesday, something specific happened in class which was quite amazing.

"Roll number eleven…" called out the old professor.

"Present sir," I replied. I was dreaming about Kaavya. A few moments later,

"Roll number 47…" came the same irritating voice.

"Present……………" I said, followed by, "…sir…" in a feeble voice, while I realized what a big blunder had happened.

Everyone's eyes turned towards me, and then towards Kaavya, who couldn't control her laughter.

My senses were out of service. For a moment I kept switching between staring at Kaavya and then the professor. After studying the situation for a moment, the professor was furious.

"What's going on? Please be attentive, or leave my class," came a strong retort from him. Young professors are usually very obsessed with themselves and end up being either too strict or too lenient. This guy belonged to the former category. The whole class burst into a silent laughter.

"What's the matter with you man…" asked Rony.

I couldn't reply to his question. I was lost in another dream. I was only partly conscious. A song was playing in the background as I wandered in an endless garden in dreamland…

'Dil tere bin kahin lagta nahi, waqt guzarta nahi…

Kya yahi pyar hai…'

That evening, Kaavya sent me a message saying that my reaction in class was both cute and ridiculous. The next day something seriously ridiculous happened in class.

"Leave me dude…you stupid jerk…" Bhalu used his massive hands to throw me away. I fell down near the next seat, unaware of what was happening. My bum was hurting, and my eyes were wide open. I began to observe what was going on around me. I glanced at the large wall clock in the lecture hall. It was five minutes past noon. The last lecture for the day was over. It was Thursday after all. Most of the students had already left the class and the rest were leaving. Bhalu was staring at me fiercely,

"Are you frigging gay?!" he shouted. I could see some guys stop and give me a dirty look as I tried to compose myself and get up.

"Uhh…what's happening here? Why did you hit me so hard?" I demanded an explanation.

"Why not? You were tugging at my arms asking me not to leave. 'Please don't go baby…my darling, I can't stay without you' that's what you were saying. You moron…" Bhalu spoke in a hurting tone. Anybody else would have felt abused, but not me. Love had numbed my senses, remember.

I got up, picked up my notebook and left without another word. I was trying to remember what had happened. After coming out of the lecture hall, everything became very clear and I laughed hard at myself. This was what had happened –

I was making love with Kaavya, in a luxurious dimly lit room somewhere in dreamland. It was an intense affair and I was keenly enjoying every part of it. Suddenly, Kaavya got up and began to leave. It was so spontaneous that I didn't understand what was happening. That was when I tried to stop her. 'Please don't go baby…my darling, I can't stay without you, you're my everything…' was all I could tell her before coming back to reality albeit I wanted to stay there, thanks to a powerful punch from Bhalu.

Today I was feeling extremely weary. The last week had been full of mysteriously uncanny experiences. I wanted to get away with this feeling. I wanted to tell Kaavya about this. And I wanted to tell her soon. I thought I could go out with her this Sunday. Yes, this Sunday would be perfect. I had heard 'Anjaana Anjaani' was the perfect movie to watch with your girlfriend (or to-be-girlfriend). Would she come with me? I needed to ask her now…

> Me: Hey, wht r u doin?
> She: Nthng, u say…
> Me: Gtng bored. I'll visit d mall on Sunday, wanna giv me company?
> She: Sure, y not!
> Me: Alrite thn, c u on Sunday evng at 5. Gn. Sd. J
> She: Yup! Gn, Tc J

I couldn't sleep that night and was completely restless the next day. 'How was I going to propose to her, How would she react', and several similar questions had filled up my mind… Maybe I would just let things unfold…

ISHQ…WHERE IT BEGAN

Finally, after waiting impatiently for several thousand seconds, that auspicious occasion arrived. I was going to meet her, *alone*. Just the two of us would be there and nobody else. I was getting excited just at the thought of it. Man! What would happen when she would actually sit beside me in a dark theatre with some romantic flick going on? It would be just awesome!

I didn't distinctly remember the time we met, and how we exactly met. How we went to the theater, how she frowned childishly when I booked corner seats, how she gracefully sat in the corner seat, and allowed me to sit on the next one. I didn't even remember what happened until the interval. I was excited as well as nervous. She would look at me several times and seeing no reaction from my side would get back to the flick. Maybe she liked Ranbir Kapoor. Frankly speaking, I didn't find the movie very interesting. But after the interval, things began becoming better…

"Dude, did she say *yes*," DKP asked me when I called him during the interval.

"No...not yet..." I said in a voice that made DKP understand the situation. I must say he was quite experienced in this game.

"Did you even ask her?" said DKP, and shortly after getting no significant reply from my side, "Aarav, did you even talk to her?" he exclaimed.

Again, there was no reply from me.

"C'mon buddy. You've got to do this, or else be a loser all the way." His words made me feel somewhat hurt. Something inside me began to accelerate. It was my heart beat. I took several deep breaths.

"Yeah, I'll do it!" I said confidently to DKP and hung up.

I entered the theater with popcorns, where she was waiting for me with folded hands.

"*Thoda late ho gaya,* sorry!" I tried to sound as realistic as I could. She took the popcorn from my hand and told me to sit. As I sat, a beautiful song played on screen and it made me feel a bit better...

> *Ab se koi khushi nahi, jiski tum wajah nahi,*
> *Ab se koi din nahi, jiski tum subah nahi...*

I looked at her, she was smiling. I put my left hand on the arm-rest which was common for both the seats. Her soft hands, which were already resting there, touched mine and generated a sensation all through my body and mind. I felt an immediate urge to cuddle up with her. Somehow, my shyness got the better of me and any scene of cuddling up was avoided. While the song came to an end, maybe even she was enjoying the sensation of being with me. Since I wasn't saying anything even remotely romantic, she took the initiative to help us get started.

"You know what. Everyone calls me by a sweet pet name. Why don't you give me a pet name too?" she sounded very happy. For a moment I kept staring into her eyes, they were beautiful. I felt as if I could spend my whole life looking at those mesmerizing eyes. She was either waiting for an answer from me, or was herself enjoying the pleasure of having me stare at her.

After a moment, I said, "Ok, how about *Sweetu*." I said shyly, trying to avoid eye contact.

"Naah! That is just soooo common. Give me another name, which can be just mine...from you," she said seductively. Maybe she really was speaking seductively or was it an effect of being so physically close to her. Whatever it was, I was enjoying it.

"What if I call you *dearie*?"

"Aaru! That is just so uncool..." her voice was so sweet. She had just called me *Aaru*. Now I needed to give her a name that could not only define her, but also my feelings for her. I wanted a name that she could keep with her for a lifetime, a name that would form her identity in my heart.

"I will call you *Ishq*..."

"*Ishq*...!! Ummm.. irritating, as well as interesting in its own right...!! I like it!" she chirped, and gently brushed her shoulder against mine.

When the movie was nearing the end, Ranbir Kapoor was holding Priyanka Chopra in his arms,

"I love you Kiara..." Ranbir said, to which I involuntarily spoke up –

"*I love you Kaavya...*"

She was lost in the movie and replied intimately,

"*...and I love you...*" in a manner similar to which Priyanka had delivered the same dialogue.

My heart skipped a beat and I had to take a really deep breath to bring a smile to my face. I was feeling out of the world. But wait, did she mean it or did she just go with the flow of the dialogues that were being played on screen. *Girls are difficult to understand.*

When the moment ended, she realized I had actually proposed to her. She didn't say anything, as if she was trying to ignore the whole part of proposal and all. For the rest of the time we either talked about school or college, or ourselves. I noted mentally that she actually liked being with me. There wasn't a single occasion when she would have hinted that she didn't like something. Maybe that happens in the beginning. I didn't know. This was my *first* experience, after all.

After the movie, we had an enjoyable munching session at Domino's. She finished one whole medium pizza all by herself. She sure was a foodie. I looked at her pizza leftovers, and then looked at her. She looked cute.

I was already holidaying with her on a beach in dreamland.

Why is dreamland such a nice place to be? How good it would be if even one percent of it could be turned into reality.

I already assumed that she liked me. But the next time, I couldn't afford to come alone with her. I was just too dumb even to talk properly. We needed more time to understand each other before she could say firmly what she had said during the movie.

We were back at the institute campus and I was reluctant to let her go.

"It was a nice evening indeed, Thanks!" she said with a wonderful smile.

"Hmmm," was all I could say!

While I was walking towards my hostel, the only words that echoed in my ear were...

"...*and I love you...*"

In the same voice, same sweet voice of my darling *Ishq*...

VICKY...

There was charm in the air, as weeks passed by. I was in love, yet again! Things seemed to be easy and simple now. My days would begin with thoughts about 'Ishq' and end with them. On alternate days, sometimes every third day and sometimes even on consecutive days, we would meet at the canteen in the evening. Lectures became more and more enjoyable. There wasn't a single lecture that I missed. I began to have bath every day. Perfume bottles began to finish faster, while my dreams became longer and longer. I would try to take her photographs in class occasionally. We began to talk on Google Talk. Everything was perfect. We had become great friends by now. She would talk about her family, her friends, the food she liked, places she had been to (and would like to be at) and almost everything else. I had begun to enjoy her company. Although I was still shy talking to her in person, I had no difficulty chatting with her on phone or the Internet. Things became simpler between us. I didn't need to plan or think what I wanted to say to her. Discussions happened more naturally. My desperation to propose to her also withered away with time. Both of us began enjoying each other's presence.

Soon, there came a time when she became irresistible. I would feel sad on days when we didn't talk. I would feel bad when she wouldn't receive my call. Things were changing. I was experiencing something I never had, something that was magical…

The month of November had just begun. The environment was turning more and more pleasant. At that time I did not know that this was the last pleasant season in my life.

9 am, 2nd November, 2010

Walking around the hostel, I came across Vicky, who was busy with his guitar. He had played in the institute fests, and was quite impressive. Moreover, he had the distinction of being the only good guitarist at the campus.

"Hey dude! What's new?" he asked, seeing me cross his room.

"Yeah, nothing actually. Can you play something for me if I ask you?" I asked. I was pretty curious about his guitar. That single thing which weighed less than five kilograms had made him a star overnight. I must also admit that I was somewhat jealous of him.

"Sure man. What do you want me to play, tell me." He got excited.

"Can you play *'Far away'*…that I love you …that I have loved you all along…" I began humming the song.

He immediately synced with what I was humming and added life to it with music from his guitar. It was amazing.

After a few minutes of random talk about girls, booze, and money, I left his room.

My personal opinion of him was fantastic. He wasn't an exhibitionist or something, as people used to say, but he was definitely a great human being and a great friend, from that day. It was the day that marked the beginning of my end.

THE PROPOSAL...

With Kaavya, time flew like a pleasant breeze. I was enjoying every moment of my life. But I hadn't proposed her yet, *formally*. I needed to do it soon, and I was aware of it. I wanted to hear her say those three magical words to me. I wanted her to melt away in a deep embrace with me. I wanted to feel her, I wanted to love her. And I wanted to do it soon.

On the eve of 31st December 2010, all four of us had an exciting party. We were just back from our semester breaks, and I had badly missed chatting with my 'Ishq'...

The other day I heard a different story about Vicky, a different one altogether.

"He has a crush on Kaavya," informed Bhalu, "Maybe you should do your part before it gets too late."

His words hinted that he wanted me to go ahead and tell Kaavya how I felt about her, officially. His primary concern was Vicky, who would constantly speak about Kaavya among his group of friends. He would often say, "In the kind of situation that we are, at IIT, you never know who's vying for whom. It's always better to do the best you can, while there is still time as well as opportunity."

He wasn't wrong, and I took his words seriously.

We had been dating for like four months now. It was a perfect time to enter into a lifetime relationship with 'Ishq', or maybe that was what I felt.

Two weeks later, we went for another movie – *Yamla Pagla Deewana*. The girl in the movie was very sweet, but not half as sweet as my cute 'Ishq'. I imagined me and 'Ishq' as the lead characters all through the movie. It was fun actually. Except that I was not a drunkard like the actor in the movie. It was a great experience, overall.

After the movie, we had pizzas at Domino's. She even paid for the pizza and shared part of my expenditure at the theatre too.

"Aarav, if we're going out frequently, it doesn't seem nice. We're almost like a couple you know!" she mentioned the word 'almost' just preceding 'couple'.

"Hmm…" I just let her do whatever she wanted to do. Usually, girls get pissed off if you don't let them do things that they want to. My serious cause of concern was just one word – *almost* – I just needed to get this word out.

We kept on chatting for some more days, wherein I would flirt with her lightly…

Kaavya: *What are you doing…*

Me: *Missing you, what else?*

Kaavya: *I had a tiring day…*

Me: ....

Kaavya: Arre we have to study a lot, unlike you guys.

Me: You mean we don't study?

Kaavya: No, but you study so you can explain stuff to me. You have a motivation behind studying, a cute and beautiful one. I have none.

Me: Leave it, what are your plans for the last weekend of January?

Kaavya: Why...Mr. A wants to take me for a movie again!

Me: Batman.......

Kaavya: Ok Batman! Which movie?

Me: Dil to Bachcha hai ji...

Kaavya: Hmm...we'll go...but promise me one thing...

Me: Kya?

Kaavya: We will have Vanilla, not Chocolate this time, at Mc' D...

Me: Ok dost. Vanilla it will be...

On 30th I would let her have the pleasure of being my girl. OK, I am exaggerating a bit. Actually, I would have the pleasure of calling her my girl. Exactly five days later, I would be the happiest person on earth.

30th January 2011, 1 am

I am chatting with Kaavya, almost on the verge of declaring my love for her...I have already changed her name from Kaavya to 'Ishq' in my messenger.

Ishq: *If you were to propose to me, I would want you to do it at an odd time of the day...*

Me: *Is it an indication that you want me to propose now, at this time itself?*

Ishq: *............. ;)*

Such an indication it was!

Me: *You know something, I have even written a poem for you. Wanna listen?*

Ishq: *Aarav...*

Me: *Ok, it's not really a poem, here's what it is...*

Ishq: *Say it Aarav, I'm waiting...*

Me: *It's been a few days since I know you, and believe me dear you have taken me into a completely new world...Where it's just you and me...Every time I talk to you, I have this wish in my heart that may our conversations just keep on going...I just want to keep listening to your voice forever...your voice is the sweetest chocolate I have ever had...Now even chocolates don't taste so sweet...whenever I talk to you, chat with you...I feel so complete...I love you... babu.. I love you...*

Ishq: *Haha...babu...*

Me: *What makes you laugh?!*

Ishq: *I want to see your face, I want to see how you're blushing.*

Me: *I'm going to sleep, but I'll be dreaming about you my darling...*

Ishq: *See you in dreams my superman!*

She went offline. I took my mobile phone and began anew –

Me: Slept?

She: Naah…

Me: You didn't answer my question…

She: I will…be patient batman!

Me: I'm waiting…

She didn't reply. Maybe she was still thinking about what to say…

I couldn't sleep at all. At six in the morning, I logged into Gtalk again. To my amazement, she was online…

Me: Hiii…

Ishq: ………..

Me: Didn't sleep? Ishq…

Ishq: You took away my sleep. I'm completely bowled over by your poems. I've become a fan of yours…

Was she kidding? I had sent her a few of my poems, and couldn't believe she had preferred reading my poems to sleeping. I was feeling out of the world. She did love me.

We went to the theater. She was quiet and blushing. She would, on numerous occasions, look at me and smile and then look away. Inside the theater, I put my hand over hers and she didn't resist. She actually liked the warmth that was created between the entangled fingers. She held onto my hand tightly, and enjoyed every pleasant part of the movie. *She is sure of her feelings, just unsure about how to say the three magic words*, that is what I thought.

After the movie, she said nothing. I felt she was ignoring me. I was confused and chose to stay quiet. I wanted to give her more time to understand my feelings for her completely. Maybe she was working out the perfect way to say 'I love you' to me. In that case, I could actually have helped her.

After reaching the campus, she quietly took the path towards the Girls' Hostel without even saying a word. She was lost in some kind of a dream. I didn't want to bother her. I wanted her to take her own sweet time and space to think about me and then let me know how she felt. Although I was quite sure that she did have similar feelings for me, I was in no hurry at all.

I had a bath, came to my room, played some music and enjoyed the moment. I was completely overjoyed after my date with 'Ishq' today.

At about fifteen minutes to midnight, I opened my mail and there was a mail from her with the subject line,

I hate you... <3

It made me smile. I opened the E-mail, as my heart missed a beat.

She had written,

"I hate you, because you like me. I hate you, because I am afraid of falling in love with you. I hate you, because, in fact, I have already fallen in love with you. But I still hate you, because I am confused about this relation..."

I smiled. I wanted to reply, I thought about it for a while and then clicked on 'Compose new mail'

Just as I was beginning to type something, she pinged me on the messenger...

Ishq: I think you love me more than I ever can. You made me feel the BEST I ever had. You have just completed my world. A million thanks to you...

Me: Yes my love, I care for you with my soul and heart...I'm trying harder and harder to believe on my destiny. Have I really got you? Or is this a dream?

And we went on chatting for about six hours. We talked about the times we had spent together, the hidden feelings we had, our past crushes, time spent in school and a lot of other things.

It was six in the morning, 'Ishq' wanted to take our conversation to dreamland now...

Me: You know something 'Ishq'...You and I have beautifully ruined our lives by deciding to live in the cage of each other's love. We're of no use to the world now, what do you say?

Ishq: Though I didn't express it but it was my wish too. Sorry for the reaction... Gimme some time, and I will be right there besides you. And I will love you like I have never loved anyone...

I was on cloud number nine. I shut down my laptop and closed my eyes. I love you 'Ishq'...I love you...

THE BREAKUP: Season 1...

The following months proved to be a roller coaster ride for me. Time flew faster than I had imagined. I was carefully balancing my time between 'Ishq' and studies. My academic performance was very close to becoming the best anyone had ever witnessed. I was working really hard. We had been for a date on 1st February itself. I just couldn't take my eyes off her. Both of us spent quality time with each other.

After that we used to go for evening walks regularly. Every evening, after dinner, we used to meet at our favorite place called 'Lovers' Crossroads'. It was named so because of the large number of couples of IIT, for whom the place was heaven. Everyone loved this place, the name of which was now abbreviated as 'LC', as it catered to the needs of all. Couples would enjoy the privacy the place offered, while those who were single would prefer to sit in some invisible corner so they could witness some hot action among highly active couples. If they were lucky, some hot single chick would accompany her committed friend and her boyfriend, showing off some attractive curves. It was their way of satisfying the animal inside them, which had become immune to porn after all this time in college.

Every time we chatted over the phone, I would send her my last message like this,

I *some text missing* u... Meri jaan...

I liked doing only two things during this time – missing her...and missing her badly.

"Love you too batman! I can't resist your absence now. I've gone mad for you, madly in love with you. Just be there... always, please......I would die without you..." she would usually say.

I wanted to gift her something very precious, something that was close to my heart. I wanted to give her something that could remind her of me, of my love for her. So after great thought, I gifted my old, cute teddy bear. It was small, brownish, and cute. She loved it so much that she actually kissed it in front of me and said, "I will just imagine it's you, and even you do the same... and all the kisses it gets, will one day be yours." And she blushed.

After a week, she went to her home. She was supposed to come after ten days...ten long days. I just wished these days would pass somehow. It was the time when I was addicted to her. I wanted her to be close to me.

One morning she sent me a nice message which I can never forget.

O my Sweet GOD! The beautiful eyes reading this SMS, have some beautiful dreams in them. Make all these dreams come true...

I replied with a modest: I love you. Have a grt day!

I had entered into an extremely serious relationship with Kaavya. I had given her a spacious bungalow in a plush location in my heart. In fact, I had given her the only place that existed. I had become so confident about the depth of our relationship that I thought of Kaavya as a member of my family. Now I wanted to settle down in life and concentrate on the larger purpose – *our future.*

In any relationship it usually happens that the level of attraction drops down significantly after some time. For me, this time was too short. She had become more than a girlfriend for me, and so I felt it was unnecessary to impress her anymore now. I felt our relationship had moved ahead of materialistic requirements and had transformed into a deep emotional connection…

♡ ♡ ♡

In March, we actually began to study together. It was just two months to go for the exams and, as usual, as a girl, she was very much concerned about her grades and stuff. She would often cite studies as a reason for not being able to come for an evening walk. I sincerely accepted the fact that the evening walk took about five hours of our time – two for the actual walk, one for the preparation before the walk, and two for the restlessness after the walk. Even after the restlessness and the feeling of being away from each other were gone, I would feel tired and almost ready for a good night's sleep, which would last no less than eight hours. So this whole concept of evening walks ate up a lot of our time. Moreover, as the novelty of LC wore off, we began to get bored with it. Not that LC became any less popular, I mean singles would still visit the place to get a glimpse of the latest hot chicks on the campus, but that was simply because a new batch, consisting one fifth of chicks out of which about one tenth were hot, joined each year.

As such, I chalked out a master plan. This is what it was –

I would first study all the subjects in depth, understand each part of the theory thoroughly, and I would do this without the knowledge of 'Ishq'. Once I was done with this, I would keep revising. A chapter which I had revised at least thrice would be ready for me to tutor her on. I would then ask her whether she had read that particular chapter. If she had already read it, I would ask her if she could help me out with some facts. If she hadn't, I would tell her that we could study it together. She would have no option, but to agree in either case. My purpose of the whole exercise, being with 'Ishq', would be served no matter how much I had to study.

This was indeed a foolproof plan. For the first trial of the plan, I chose to do the chapter on 'Diodes' in the course 'Basic Electronics'. It was a tough chapter, at least for me at that time, and very important for upcoming semesters as mentioned in the syllabus. I read the chapter about seven or eight times until I had learnt the diagrams and stuff by heart. I even practiced all the constructions and problems as though I would be sitting for a job interview soon. It took me about four days of consistent studies, and missing out on evening walks, to complete that damn thing. But when I was done, I was quite satisfied.

I decided to call her up, and schedule a two-three hour session in the pre-evening time.

"Hi!" she said cheerfully.

"Hi...what's up?"

"Missing you badly my *jaan*. Preparing for minor exams..."

"Hmmm...have you done the chapter on diodes yet?"

I was expecting her to say no, because then I would get more time to spend with her. Maybe we could have split sessions spanning over several days. That would be absolutely perfect.

"Umm...just the first few slides done, what about you?"

'What the heck! What slides?' I wanted to ask. I had spent my entire time with a book so thick that it's volume could actually hold about eight liters of water, only to find out that there was something still remaining!

"Where did you get the slides from?"

"I got them from a senior, she was kind enough plus she wanted to delete them as they took up lot of unnecessary space on her laptop..." she explained.

"But what will you do with slides? You don't have a laptop, do you?" I enquired.

"I put them on Suchi's..."

An idea struck me instantly...

"Why don't you get those slides and we can read them

on my laptop, at about five in the evening, in the garden near Block B?"

"Are you sure?" she was just being too formal.

"Of course…yes, will you be there? 5 pm sharp?" I wanted to confirm.

"Yes batman! I'll be there!" she giggled, as if she had understood my plans.

"Alright then, see you in the evening sweetheart."

"Bye…" she said sweetly.

I hung up. My plan had worked. Finally…

24th April, 2011

It was the usual sort of Sunday, except that exams were supposed to begin in a few days. I had performed exceptionally well in most of the subjects earlier, and had to do just the same in the coming exams. I was prepared, thanks to 'Ishq' and she was prepared too, thanks to me. My idea had worked wonders not just for me, but also for her and our relationship. The more time I spent with her, the more I loved her.

"Aaru, I'm nervous…I need some help in philosophy and human values…" she told me during our evening walk. We were probably the only couple who could manage to spend time in walks even during exams. The reason was pretty simple. We had prepared well in advance for the upcoming exams. We had actually brought meaning to our relationship, thereby proving that a relationship, when true, could be very very constructive…

"What's the big deal in philosophy?" I remarked.

It was an easy subject. It required just plain memorizing of stuff and that is what I told her.

"Ok let's see what we have here...Umm...common terminal values...Wealth, Inner harmony, mature love, pleasure, true friendship, an exciting life, social recognition... How are we supposed to memorize all this?" she asked.

"See, it's quite easy actually. Terminal values refer to what you want at the end of your life. I mean, what you would like to possess, when you can say that you're done with most of your duties and responsibilities in life..."

She thought about it for a while. Then she looked at me, and smiled. Maybe she was beginning to understand.

"Umm...let me see...what I would want when...OK..." she got excited and then began listing things she wanted to achieve in life...

"Wealth, alright...and love, that's true. Pleasure, social recognition, friendship, exciting day to day life, peace..."

Her face seemed to be glowing with happiness. She had no difficulty recalling all the terminal values.

"Wow...you're amazing. Is this the way you did it too?"

Her question was a bit difficult to answer. I paused for a while, and scratched my forehead.

"Yeah, you can say that," I said, trying to sound cool. She began to look for some other part which she found difficult.

"Except that, instead of all this, what I want from life is

something very precious. In fact, it is my own requirement for terminal values…"

She closed her book and began listening keenly. I paused again. This time she fixed her gaze on me and raised her eyebrows, expecting me to continue. And so I did…

"When I am done with most of the duties and responsibilities in life, I want just…"

"Say it…*na*…" she dragged the words in such a way that it made me blush.

"You…I just want you…I just want my 'Ishq'…"

She smiled at me, I smiled in return. She kept the book, which was in her hand all through this time, on the ground below a nearby tree and embraced me. Resting her head over my chest, she felt comfortable and cozy. We didn't say a single word for about a minute, just enjoyed that feeling. My eyes opened, as her head rose up, and she looked into them, from just a couple of inches away.

"I don't think I will ever be able to love you as much as you do Aaru…"

A drop of moisture was released from her twinkling eyes. It fell on my shirt, just near my heart. Although my skin didn't feel it, the droplet had created an impact which was significant. It made the ocean of her love expand several times, and I was completely submerged in it. There was no way I could ever get out of it, and I never even wanted to.

"Don't worry 'Ishq', you're the best. I love you so much… that you won't have to love me! Loving you gives me strength, caring for you gives me the confidence to face any situation in life. I just can't imagine life without you. I love you," I said, as I moved my arms around her and held her tightly. She held me tightly too.

"Mmmm…we have exams darling, we need to study," she said in a dreamy voice. She probably didn't mean it. I didn't want her to spoil the moment by talking about values and crap.

"*Naah*…Just let this moment continue forever." I pulled her closer towards me. She closed her eyes, and…

We kissed…

Tides of emotion and love ran down our bodies as we submitted ourselves to each other. Our feelings sublimed into deep threads of pure trust and care.

After a few more minutes, it was time for us to go back to our hostels. She picked up the philosophy notes and began to leave. I held her hand, urging her to wait for a few more minutes.

"I need to go baby, exams from Tuesday…pleaseee *jaane do*…"

She tugged at my arms like a small child, looking unimaginably cute. It was a moment of infinite bliss. I released her hand, and let her go. I stood still at that place, looking at her until she disappeared…

♡ ♡ ♡

As I said, I wanted to settle down then. I wanted to concentrate on the larger purpose in life and I wanted 'Ishq' to do the same. I wanted her to understand how important it was for us to study, and so I decided to not meet her daily. Moreover, since it was exam time, I wanted her to study well. I met her just once, a day before exams.

"Listen, we need to take this more maturely," I said, caressing her hands with mine.

"Huh…" she indicated her disinterest.

"From now on, we won't be meeting daily. We can meet once or twice a week, not more than that…"

"Huh…" she was in no mood to listen.

"C'mon, don't act like a child…" I took both her hands in mine.

"Huh…" she said and left.

"Ok, do well in exams baby. All the best!"

"Huh…" she said. Then she looked at me, smiled wryly and walked away.

THE VICKY EFFECT...

Kaavya was sitting alone in a canteen, with a sullen face. She had coffee on her table, but looked disinterested. There was no one else in the canteen as nobody wanted to screw up their exams, not Aarav especially. She, however had different things in mind.

"One cold coffee," said a guy, at the counter. Kaavya turned to look at him. He was handsome.

Taking his coffee, he looked for a place to sit, confused because there were many. He spotted her sitting in a lonely corner table. They smiled.

"Hi!" they said, at the same time.

Her face brightened for a moment and then went back to the sullen state. She knew Vicky as they were in the same class. They were nothing more than classmates, until that day perhaps...

"What's up?" he asked.

"Nothing much, you say..."

"Gearing up for my performance in the college rock band next week, I'm the lead guitarist!"

Her eyes gleamed. How she loved rock performances. She smiled again.

"I'm sure you'll like my performance…"

"Only if Mr. Guitarist ensures that I get a front seat…" her face brightened again, and it didn't fade this time.

"Done. Front seat. Next week. Sharp at 7pm. New open air theater," he assured.

THE BREAKUP – SEASON 1 (CONTD..)

About a week later, exams had ended, and we had our first breakup. She couldn't handle the issue of not meeting daily. Since I used to meet her after a few days, I used to have lot of expectations. I wanted our encounters to be passionate. But she was adamant. One day when I asked her to meet me at the canteen, she refused. Even though I tried a lot to convince her, she didn't agree. I got frustrated a bit, and declared a break up. I thought it would help her realize what I actually wanted. And it did.

So I had stopped sending her greetings in the morning or the night. I had severed all contacts between me and her for a few days. In fact, I had switched off my phone. Somewhere, I felt she was acting as a drug for me. I was intoxicated due to her. But I wanted to get myself back. So I did not send her any message for five consecutive days, after which she gave up and sent me a message,

He wanted me to grow up, n I used 2 refuse, until d day
he stopped sending me msgs, while I ws w8ng impatiently
4 his msags...n m still w8ng...

I received it as soon as I switched on my phone. Maybe she had sent it much earlier. I felt a deep urge to reply immediately. Although I tried my best to avoid replying to her, my hand involuntarily picked up the phone and a reply was sent –

I too wanna hold ur hand, b in ur arms... wanna
b loved by u 4evr... Dis distance is nw unbearable...
wanna c u... Lv u... Kiss u..

One part of me regretted having sent that message while another part was overjoyed. It was an unexplainable feeling inside me. Within a minute she replied,

I wish d days go faster till d day I gt 2 b in ur arms
nd 1ce dat day cums may d days go as slow as possible
so dat I may b dere 4ever..

I wanted to call her now. Without waiting further I dialed her number... She picked up the phone immediately.

"Hey!!!" her voice confirmed that she was indeed glad talking to me after such a long time.

"Friendship, Kiss, long-term relationship, an apology, a chance to be best friends, a hug...be my best friend..." I said. She reciprocated in a similar fashion,

"I love it when my fingers are entangled in yours and my head on your chest, listening to your heart beat. It makes me feel so safe, like nothing bad could happen to me...ever..."

I was again lost in her love. She had, within seconds, bridged the gaps between us with subtle ease.

"I have realized in these few days 'Ishq', what love exactly is, and how much you mean to me. And it's not only me; it's always 'us'..."

"Yes, I felt a magic in the air, when you were around! I felt life is so nice, when I was in your arms. I felt heavenly, when you held me tight! I felt pure, when you kissed me. I feel secure, when I think I'm yours...Love you a lot Batman!"

After this we talked casually for a few minutes. She was happy that we were back on track. It wasn't really a breakup, but I felt like that for five whole days. So I could say that it was indeed a breakup. I don't know the reason for the change in her behavior, the way she would express disinterest, before the breakup, but I felt for sure that something was wrong in our relationship, for the first time now...

REENA...

"So he didn't come to meet you, right?" asked Reena.

Kaavya nodded. She didn't seem to be particularly happy.

"You know what. Vicky is way better than Aarav. He's absolutely dashing. He cares for you. He replies to all your texts unlike Aarav. And he gave you front row seats at the rock band competition…" added Reena. She was an average-looking girl, but a smart one indeed. Rony liked her a lot. In fact, he got his bike just to woo her. But that is a different story altogether. So we'll get to that later.

"You must be kidding. I am with Aarav, OK. I am not thinking about Vicky in *that* way…" said Kaavya.

"Alright. Leave that aside. We need to go for dinner, remember?"

"Hotel Royal Palace? Again?" asked Kaavya.

"Yeah, I love the food they serve. C'mon, quick…" demanded Reena.

Hotel Royal Palace was a great place to dine. They used to

serve some nice south Indian dishes. Kaavya sat opposite to Reena at the table which they had already booked. They ordered some food and began to talk.

"So, what else, what's with Aarav?" said Reena.

"He wants *us* – me and himself – to concentrate on studies. That means we'll be meeting not more than twice a week…"

"I know that sweetheart. I thought you broke up with him," said Reena.

"No. I mean, yes, we did break up. But we're back together again…"

Reena smiled and drank some water.

"You know what. This studies and all is crap. I'm telling you this guy is too serious with matters of heart…"

"I know. But I like him. I think he just needs some space and things will be alright…"

"Yeah, whatever…"

Just then, Rony entered the dining hall and with him entered Vicky. Rony had, in fact, planned this out. He knew Reena was coming there, so he landed there too in hope of sharing a table. But since he didn't want to come across as a despo, he took Vicky along. Why he didn't take Aarav along is still a big mystery. He, however, intentionally or unintentionally, hadn't pre-booked a table.

"Hey girls, do you mind sharing the table?" Rony asked politely, facing towards Reena. She looked at Kaavya. They both smiled and then Reena spoke.

"OK…"

Rony now had the option to sit beside Reena or opposite her, beside Kaavya. Since it was not his first encounter with Reena, he found it better to sit on the chair beside Kaavya. So, Rony faced Reena and logically, Vicky faced Kaavya. And then the talking began…

"You know this watch is from Paris. My aunt had gifted me on my 16th birthday…" were Rony's first words.

As they continued talking, slowly the focus turned towards relationships. All through this time, it was just Rony who was doing all the talking. Reena would occasionally just smile and say things like, "Ohh!", "Really!", "Amazing!" which was enough to fuel Rony into continuing his nonsense. But when it turned to relationships, Kaavya began listening carefully, and so did Vicky.

"What qualities do you want in a guy?" Rony asked Reena.

"Umm…lemme see…he must be smart, handsome…"

Kaavya was gazing at Vicky and listening to Reena…very attentively.

"And…" Rony said.

"and…I don't care about his studies but he must be famous. He must be a rockstar!" cried Reena.

Vicky realized that Kaavya's eyes were fixed at him. He became a bit nervous. He was confused about his feelings for Kaavya and didn't want to mess things up.

Kaavya turned her eyes away. But Reena's words echoed in her mind…Rockstar…famous…rockstar…famous…

Rony continued to try wooing Reena, while Reena did her best at dodging him. Vicky and Kaavya remained submerged in the ocean of each other's thoughts.

That dinner at Royal Palace proved to be a turning point in the lives of three people. Kaavya, Vicky and...

...

...

...

ME.

THE BREAKUP: Season 2…

May 2011

Soon after that hotel incident, which I was unaware of, we had our Second breakup. Same issue – she didn't come to meet me again.

"I am having a severe headache Aarav. Can we meet later?" she asked over the phone. We hadn't met since four days and I seriously wanted to meet her.

"C'mon 'Ishq', please come. I'll make you feel better… please…" I pleaded.

"I'm sorry baby. Later, OK. I need to sleep today…"

It was just 9 pm, and she wanted to sleep. I felt really frustrated.

"You know what 'Ishq', I love you. Please come…" I tried again.

"Aarav. This won't work…"

I so hated that line. It was the second time she was saying 'This won't work'. Hearing this line from 'Ishq' had a very negative effect on me. I felt devastated. She ended the call without saying another word.

I stood speechless…

♡ ♡ ♡

For one whole month we didn't talk to each other. Since she had switched off her phone, I had switched off mine too, and the result was disastrous, at least for me. To escape the gloomy atmosphere at the institute, I went home. But it couldn't change my help me much. Mild feelings of ending my life had begun taking shape in my mind, which was too preoccupied with 'Ishq' at that time.

The month of June proved to be a month when my weight decreased by almost five kilograms. I was only about fifty-five earlier. Not even slightly muscular, with about average height. Due to reduced intake of food, my body was struggling for energy. I would spend days without going out for even a short while. My school friends were totally pissed off by this behavior of mine. Amit and Vishal were the closest ones, but I had still not told them about my relationship with 'Ishq'. In fact, at that time there was nothing much to tell. So I chose to keep mum about me and 'Ishq'. But close friends never fail to get hints…

"Man, are you in love? Tell me seriously," asked Amit over the phone, "and I'm standing in the compound of your building dude."

I looked out of the window to see if he was lying. He wasn't.

"No, actually…" I tried to explain him about the love part, but on hearing a 'no' he ended the call and shouted loudly.

"Then are you joining us for a cricket match…"

"C'mon buddy, I know you will," added Vishal.

I didn't want to let my friends down, but I didn't feel like doing anything. I refused to play the game and this made them go nuts.

The next day Vishal and Amit came straight to my room and, without any notice, poured a bucket-full of water over me when I opened the door.

"Bloody Asshole…Motherf…" I was just about to say something really embarrassing when my Mom came in sight. I think she missed the 'hole' part, otherwise I would've been dumped into it. Forget 'Ishq', forget Amit and Vishal, forget the whole world! I would've been in deep shit if my mouth would have emitted a few more syllables.

"Mom?!" I said shockingly.

She broke into laughter, and soon my friends joined in. I was being made fun of in front of my mom. My entire body was completely drenched. One bucket is hell lot of water.

Seeing mom laugh made me smile too. For a moment all my worries disappeared. I felt really happy. After mom left to work in the kitchen, Vishal put his arms on my shoulder and said, "How was the feeling of getting wet, eh? I'm sure you just loved it!" He said this with an extra emphasis on 'loved' trying to sound seductive. I laughed hard. Friends are actually far better companions than girlfriends. I mean, that is what I felt at that moment.

It was an amazing time. I watched some serials and some movies. After a long time, I watched porn, just to show Amit that I got access to high-def content at my hostel. He was amazed at the quality of porn, and made a very funny remark, "So even your lappy gets wet by these?"

It made me remember the times when we used to watch porn secretly. We used to get DVDs from a guy, for hundred bucks each. Once, a friend, who was co-incidentally quite well-built, was getting all desperate. He wanted to watch porn badly. He said he hadn't watched any for a month or so. I felt one month wasn't really a big deal, as I really didn't watch much. So this guy got a DVD, for one hundred bucks. He told his dad that a group of friends were having a night out for studying at another friend's place. So about six guys had gathered together, and they were pretty excited about the DVD. More so, because it had the two magical characters, 'HD', written on it. The mere look of 'HD' was getting them a hard on, as Vishal said when he later narrated the whole episode to me. All of them had gathered there. One of them had even got headphones because he wanted to 'observe' the sounds clearly. The DVD went inside. The sound of the spinning disc also got them excited. They had become impatient. Finally the television screen lit up. For a moment it was blue. It remained blue for another moment, during which a couple of guys felt it was such a turn off. At last a message was displayed on the screen –

THIS DISC IS BLANK

I only knew that the DVD seller was admitted to a hospital next day for almost a week. He was badly bruised in parts of his body which deemed 'private'. I don't need to explain it further, the rest is history...

♡ ♡ ♡

When you begin staying in a hostel, especially an IIT hostel, the behavior of parents at home changed completely. You are treated like a prince at home. Everything is at your disposal. You can eat, sleep, go out, enjoy, watch TV, or do just about anything you fancy and nobody will tell you a word. Moreover, during holidays, you don't even have to worry about going back to college, so it's much merrier. For me, however, the home environment could do very little to change my mood.

The next week was fun. I played with friends, watched movies, and went to parks. I tried my best to forget 'Ishq' completely. But it wasn't so easy. As July began, I felt like going back to the hostel. This feeling was a result of Rony's message that he had arrived at the hostel and it was absolutely empty.

"You can roam about freely like a lion…I feel like I'm the king of this place. I can do whatever I want man!"

I assumed Rony was drunk. Also, he mentioned that he had done a miraculous workout as a result of which he looked like a film star.

I wanted to see what that moron had done and wanted to get away from the environment at home. So I decided to go back to the hostel on 8th July. I began packing my stuff, and left for reaching out to my second home…

DRASTIC CHANGES...

When I reached IIT, the first look of Lovers' Crossroads brought back memories of me and 'Ishq' all afresh. As I strolled down the path along the gardens, I realized how beautiful the place was.

The hostel was really quiet and empty.

"Finally our lover boy has arrived!" shouted Bhalu. I hadn't expected him to be there too. But you never knew about Rony's plans. He always did the unexpected. After a while he arrived at the place where Bhalu and I were discussing random things. Some were useful, such as Rony's latest love interest from Ludhiana, and some were useless, such as the semester results. I had scored a 9.1 on the CGPA scale. 'Ishq' was not far behind with 8.37, which was relatively higher than most of the girls. I had almost topped the class. But I was not happy...

"Hi...Assholes!"

I looked at Rony, and couldn't believe at what I saw. He looked completely different.

"Un-fucking-believable!" I cried...

"Man, he looks like *one of us* now…finally…" Bhalu laughed it off.

But what he said was right. Rony had changed completely. Either he had worked out very hard, or he had simply got some expensive tummy tuck or something. In either case, he looked unbelievably fantastic.

We went out to the mall in the evening, and had a lot of fun. But all through the time, I had only 'Ishq' on my mind. I was feeling sad, really sad. Rony did try to cheer me up. On several occasions, he cracked filthy jokes, aimed towards me and 'Ishq'. I, somehow, managed to hide my pain and anguish for 'Ishq' from my friends.

When we came back that evening, I was very tired, both from roaming in the city and worrying about problems with 'Ishq'. I decided to give her a call. I dialed her number, and waited for the ring. During this time, I was worried about how she would react to the whole thing. I didn't want to piss her off again. I just wanted to talk to her, listen to her soothing voice, and go to sleep. I just wanted to know if my 'Ishq' was all OK.

'The number you are trying to call is currently switched off…'

I tried to call again.

'…out of coverage area. Please try after some time…'

I tried to call a few more times but got the same message. It was outrageous. After a while, when I found no other option, I felt I should send her a message. She could receive it the next time she switched on her phone, even for a couple of minutes. So I typed in a message,

Hope aal izz well at home. Dnt think much, evrything
is fair for love and Ishq!

The message got sent, but was not delivered. I was looking continuously at my phone screen for a couple of minutes. Still, it was not delivered.

I decided to send another message.

And 'gud mrng' nd 'gud nyt' for each and evry day
till u cum back 2 clg. Wil miss u a lot...

It got sent again, but no delivery acknowledgement.

I logged into my Facebook and looked at her pictures. She looked beautiful, and it made me miss her more and more. Her pictures reminded me of the times when I used to try taking her pictures secretly. Skimming through 'Photos of Kaavya', as Facebook liked to put it, I came across a sketch in which she was tagged. The sketch actually belonged to my profile, but appeared in that area because of the tag. The picture now had 100+ likes and close to 200 comments. I didn't remember the context, but I still remembered the day when I had drawn her sketch, in class. It had been my first attempt at sketching but she didn't know it...

It was the month of January and I didn't remember the date. She was sitting in the first row, like most girls and I was in the third. The lecture hall was arranged in the form of a theater with seats in each row at a raised height than the previous one. I could gaze at her without her knowing about it. That day, she was wearing a bluish top and jeans. It was some boring lecture, as usual and she was taking notes, like most other silly girls. Since I could not make out what was going on during the lecture, I decided to make good use of some things.

I had free time, blank sheets and, surprisingly, a working pen… and I had 'Ishq', which completed the scenario. I set out to draw a sketch of her. I started with fine strokes that depicted her hair, her profile, her shoulders, her curves…

I was sitting in a position from where her profile was visible. So I needed to be extra careful while drawing her face. In fact, only her right profile would show. Once an outline was ready, I began working on the hair. I felt it was somewhat logical to draw from top to bottom, left to right, just like reading. Another thing is that, while drawing this way, you never have to rest your hand on the finished area of the drawing, in case you are right-handed for that matter. I had to pay too much attention on her ponytail, as I had to make it attractive. It was the only thing that had the potential to catch everyone's attention, so I had to make it as mysterious as possible. Her hair took a large part of my time, but I was working consistently.

Suddenly, DKP poked me with his elbow. I looked up. Another lecture had begun and the professor was about to call out my roll number.

"Thanks…" I told DKP.

After getting my presence recorded, I continued working on the hair, and then switched to her face and shoulders.

Although I was not completely done with her hair, I switched temporarily to her shoulders, which took lesser time, as there was lesser detail. Now I had to concentrate on her right profile. I had to delicately draw her eyelids, and cheeks. Once done with the upper part of her cheek, I drew her nose. Her lips were moving constantly, but somehow I visualized them being still and drew them to the best of my ability. I was concentrating as much as possible, on every single detail that I saw.

At last, at the end of the third consecutive lecture, I was done with my first sketch of my beautiful and heavenly, the only and only, 'Ishq'…

After coming back from class, I uploaded that image on Facebook. Due to my inexperienced strokes, it was difficult to make out who the girl in the picture was. Only I knew, and probably some of the girls, that only 'Ishq' sported a ponytail that day. From that day, I have never seen her sporting a ponytail. She had explained it earlier that she didn't want anyone to know that I was making a sketch of her. Somehow, people already knew it, but never mentioned it.

I kept staring at that picture for almost two hours, thinking about the day when I had made it. She was completely floored by my effort. She said she loved me. And my biggest mistake…I even believed her…

SUCHI...

Suchi was a very important chapter in my life. Since now we are heading towards a rougher patch of my life, I felt it is best to narrate about Suchi here. Her real name was Suchita and we used to call her Suchi. She was a fun-loving, cute girl. I shouldn't forget to mention that I once had a crush on her. That was when Nivedita had broken my heart. But since DKP had already wooed her, I felt it was best if I bury my feelings, however small they may be, and move ahead. So later on, we became the best of friends. I used to share every small thing with her.

We used to talk about our relationships. She also became friends with 'Ishq' maybe because of DKP and me. She always supported me when I needed it most. When I had my first breakup with 'Ishq', it was Suchi who helped me understand my relationship with 'Ishq' and get back to her. We usually chatted over the internet, and discussed a lot of things.

She was more like a sister to me. We used to share our playlists, talk about 'Ishq', DKP and ourselves, and have lots of fun. When I faced any confusion regarding 'Ishq', I turned to Suchi for support. One day, we were discussing casually about our love lives,

"And I've begun writing a novel too. But stopped writing after two pages..." I told her once on Gtalk.

"Wow! Your love story?" she asked.

"Yeah, but don't tell anyone. I'm telling just you..."

"Ohh...OK, not even DKP?"

"No...it's TOP SECRET..."

"Even I had once wanted to write my diary but then I dropped the idea thinking about the consequences if someone reads it..." said Suchi.

"Yes, that issue is always there. But it feels nice when you write it out..."

"Hmmm..."

"And should I tell you the title of my novel?" I asked her.

"Yes...tell me..."

"Third and the last...how is it?"

"Seems nice, but can get better I think..." she suggested.

"Do you know the meaning of this title?"

"Yes. I'm not stupid. You had three breakups right..."

"Great. You have a nice memory...and I have written something for the back cover too..."

"Ohh...show me..."

"Here it is...How many times can you strike a heart with a knife? Or let me put this question in a slightly different manner. How many times would it hurt when continuously struck with knife? When does the pain start vanishing? Or does it even stop getting hurt? I know the answer. Do You?"

"Umm…not that great…" she remarked.

"Awww…."

"You can write a bit better…"

"Yea, even I felt the same. Ok, I'll try to improve…"

And in that way, we used to discuss a lot of things. Suchi was undoubtedly my best friend, second only to DKP…

THE BREAKUP: SEASON 3...

I woke up in the morning at eight, the next day. I was still restless. Sleeping didn't help me ease my pain anymore. It only made it more severe, because every day I was reminded how big a failure I was.

Perhaps, the only good thing that happened today was the receipt of delivery acknowledgements of the messages that I had sent 'Ishq' last night. I tried dialing her number again. This time her phone ringed, at least on my side...

"You did nothing...maybe, but that's your mistake. But one day Mr. Virani, I would completely understand you and your ways. But one day you will have to pay for what you have done..." she sounded serious at one moment and chuckled at another. I was not prepared for this.

"I...don't want to talk...leave me...alone," I spoke with hesitation. I was taken aback at what she had just said, even if it was just a joke.

"Actually I was kidding *jaanu*. And I thought you would become sad and then I will surprise you, but it went all wrong and I got trapped in my own plan...Shit! But seriously there's nothing you did about me. Seriously, now you understand why I was sorry." She made a sarcastic remark again. Maybe she thought I was kidding about not wanting to talk to her. How badly mistaken she was…

"Leave. Me. Alone I said…" and I disconnected the call. Her message arrived almost instantly.

Pls talk 2 me…

I felt bad about having disconnected the call. I dialed her number again.

"Hello…I'm sorry dear, I was seriously having a tough time, and I was missing you like hell…"

"It's alright. Nobody's perfect. I was thinking a lot about myself and that's the reason I had become pessimistic. And that is the reason I was not able to comprehend with your reaction," she explained.

My reaction? Now this was something I was not prepared for. Almost in reflex, I blurted out,

"Ok, leave me, don't talk to me…I won't talk to you…"

And with that I disconnected the call again.

A minute later, her number flashed on my screen. I didn't have enough strength to reject this call, but somehow, I did.

A moment later, she called up again. This time, I had to take the call.

"Alright, don't talk to me. I deserve it. I'm sorry you made me your choice. Love you. Bye…"

She was the one to disconnect the call this time. But maybe

she was not able to handle this, and about forty minutes later, I got her call again.

I was firm on my decision now. I rejected the call. She called up again. I rejected her call six times...

Plzz Aaru... I need u... I beg of u... plzz...

I deleted the message as soon as it arrived. She sent another one,

Aarav... Plz chat wid me... jst once, I won't ever ask u 2 talk again.
I promise. Bt plzz talk 2 me, atleast 1ce...Plzzz...

I had to call her now...

"I don't understand what you want from me, at the moment. I think we both should give this some time. Everything will be perfect...believe me..." I had become rational in my behavior towards her.

"Hmm...Hope so...don't leave me...please..."

"I won't, but just don't become too selfish. Take care..."

"Bye..."

I was nearly crying out. I didn't even leave my room the next day. I skipped breakfast, lunch and dinner, altogether...

When she came back to the institute, in August, we couldn't help meeting each other. The first time, we behaved as if we had almost forgotten about everything and things were back to normal.

"I really missed you…"

"You have no idea how much I missed you batman…"

Now I didn't find it loving when she called me by names. Although we talked less, we made sure we didn't talk about the bad part much. The first week of third semester passed without much conflict. She was trying her best to maintain peace. Maybe the home environment had made her feel different. We had resumed our evening walks. Everything was perfect except one thing. There was some issue with her Gtalk…

Initially I thought it would be a minor issue, but it was not. The whole episode, which happened towards the end of August, shattered me completely. Here's what happened…

For almost ten days, we were not able to chat on Gtalk as she said there were some problems and she was not able to log in. I offered to check her laptop and sort out the problem but she, somehow, declined. I suggested she could take the laptop to someone senior and maybe she could help. She didn't even try that. But the reality was something else. It was something DKP found out after lot of investigation and effort.

One day, DKP came into my room and said,

"Dude, see if Kaavya is online…"

"Why…what happened?"

"Dude just check man…"

I logged into Gtalk. I scanned the whole list of online friends. 'Ishq' was not there, so she was surely offline.

"She's offline, see…"

"Dude...try entering her name..."

I couldn't figure out what he was saying. So, I just did what he said. In the search bar, I typed 'Kaavya' and there were no results.

"See, she's offline, her name doesn't even come in the search results..."

I hadn't finished saying it when I realized what a big blunder it was.

"A friend who is offline will still appear in the search results, got something?" his words made sense now. Absolute sense...

"You mean to say..." I stopped for a while as I understood she had blocked me. DKP nodded and looked at me. I was speechless and could only utter – "But why..."

"Man, she's not even there in my chat list, or on anyone else's, but that isn't the bad part yet..."

I got confused again. One thing was sure that she had blocked me, and probably DKP, and some others from F4 too, but if this was not bad, then I was really afraid to hear what was...

"I just came from Vicky's place. He was playing his guitar. I quietly entered his room. After he finished playing, I heard Kaavya's voice from his laptop. She said 'nice', and then they giggled..."

"What the f..."

With Gtalk you can make voice calls for free over the internet to people with a Google account. But it was difficult for me to believe that she had actually blocked me and was talking to Vicky. It seemed like impossible, but I had to believe DKP.

I got up from my chair. "I need to sleep," I told DKP. Without further discussion, he left the room. I lay on my bed thinking about the whole thing. I thought I should call her and ask about this. But I thought I should wait and let the situations unfold.

....NEXT DAY

"Is your Gtalk alright now?" I somehow missed my tone, and said it in a way that sounded suspicious.

"Why…yeah, yes actually…just yesterday evening…" she tried her best to clarify.

I don't remember the time I spent with her in the two months that followed, but it probably wasn't any good. It wasn't really the way it should have been. She would talk to me, but not with full sincerity. She would listen to me, but not with full attention. My feelings were playing with my heart. 'Ishq' was playing with my feelings. My heart was actually enjoying the fact that it was being played with. Although I was dead sure that 'Ishq' was cheating on me, I would never believe that until she told me upfront. Until that time, I would love her like I did. Even after she declared that she no longer loved me, I wouldn't be able to forget her. It is impossible for me to leave 'Ishq' now. The only thing I could do is…QUIT…

EMOTIONAL CONFRONTATIONS...

Since I was not able to face the harsh truth that 'Ishq' had lost interest in me, I continued to burn in the heat of my own emotions. I was already weak, physically, and now my mental stability was getting affected badly. I was facing deep emotional trauma after 'Ishq' showed signs of cheating.

The month of October marked the onset of winter season. I had contracted cold, was emotionally down and add to that, I had hurt my hand by hitting it to the wall of my room. I was upset with the Gtalk issue. It was bleeding. I couldn't sleep that night. Although DKP came to know about my condition only by 3 am in the night, I still hesitated to let him know what had happened between 'Ishq' and me.

"Listen buddy, I'll get you some medicines and something to eat at 6 am. Don't worry," he tried to console me. DKP sometimes acted like my brother. I loved him for this. I felt he was so lucky to have Suchi in his life who was equally caring and loving. I wished 'Ishq' too would love me like that.

But I was getting blow after blow…let alone wishes getting true!

♡ ♡ ♡

The clock struck 6. DKP got ready to go out and get something for me to eat, plus medicines.

I waited for about an hour. I was thinking about 'Ishq' all the time. When DKP returned he had another blow ready for me...

"Dude...here you go. Take these tablets; they'll ease your pain..." said DKP.

I took one of the tablets which was yellowish and gulped it down with water. Yellow was her favourite color...

Just when I picked up the second tablet, DKP spoke,

"And by the way, I saw your sweetheart...and Vicky too. They were roaming around near the gardens..."

My eyes opened wide. DKP was saying this casually. He did know something was wrong, but he didn't know that, in fact, everything was wrong.

The background of this story was something like this –

[In Vicky's room]

"I really like her and I think even she does, but I don't know if I should move ahead because I feel I am betraying my friend Aarav..." said Vicky.

"Buddy...*Pyar kiya to darna kya*...just go ahead and tell her what you feel about her..." said Rony.

"But..."

"No But, *lekin, kintu* or *parantu*...you will tell her about your feelings tomorrow itself..." declared Rony.

Vicky was shocked.

"Tomorrow? But how?"

"Leave that to me dude…tomorrow morning, Reena is gonna come along with Kaavya to the gardens. You come along with me, simple…"

"You think so…" he sounded confused.

"Yep man! Just give it your best shot!"

Vicky felt elated, and went to sleep…

In the morning…

"Hi…" said Vicky.

"Hiii," said Kaavya, looking visibly happy, "Where's Rony?"

"I tried a lot to wake him up, but he simply didn't…"

"Ohh…same with Reena, tried a lot but couldn't wake her up…"

And in that way, everything turned in favour of Vicky, and Kaavya too…I was hurt, sick, depressed, and 'Ishq' was happily enjoying her time with Vicky. She didn't even feel it necessary to let me know what was going on between her and Vicky. It was simply unbearable…

I had two options – to face the truth and move on, or give up and die. And believe me, the second option seemed to the easier one…

ISHQ DIVERSIFIED...

"**D**on't you love me?"

"I do…But…"

"Then why don't you like to spend time with me. Why is it that only I want to hold your hand, not you?"

There was an irritating silence in the air.

"Aarav…I…"

She wanted to say something but was hesitant. Her head was still bowed, her eyes firmly fixed on the floor.

"Why don't you want to share your problems with me? Why don't you feel comfortable with me?"

Although I was demanding a part of my own right on her, she took it rather differently. I began losing my patience…

"I think you're not able to understand me. Maybe I am not up to your expectations. I am too big a responsibility for you…"

She raised her head. Her desperation was visible in the form of tearful eyes, ready to pour. Her expression fluctuated between guilt and anger. For a moment, I thought I had won the battle. The next moment, I had lost it. I had lost everything...

"You know what. I love Vicky more than you..."

She was breathing heavily. My breathing had stopped. In fact, for a while, everything had stopped. My brain refused to react to this. My weak heart somehow convinced my brain that she was just kidding, just to hurt me. Was I a fool? Yes, maybe I was. I was trying to cover up a wound that would never heal, ever.

Gathering some courage, I put my hand around her shoulders,

"Come, let's walk." I said, getting up and waiting for her.

She looked at me. Her expressions became clearer now. She didn't like my touch anymore.

"*Main mazak nahi kar rahi.* I was feeling guilty every single second of my life. I was dying from inside..."

I knew I had lost everything. For the sake of my love for her, I didn't cry out. I stayed calm, still listening to her.

"I used to like him since our first year. When I did realize my love for him, I was committed to you. Eventually I got attached to you..."

Even a slight indication that she still loved me was a reason enough for me to live. But her next words made me feel as worthless as a used up condom.

"But now it is difficult for me to hide this feeling. And when you began to care for me, and caress me like a child, I began to suffocate in my own feelings. I felt as if I am cheating on you. I can't handle this anymore Aarav, I can't handle this anymore…"

I moved away from her. She was almost crying. Her eyes turned again to the floor and remained fixed there for a long while. My heartbeat was racing ahead of time. I could see my future…my bright dark future…

When you love someone more than they deserve, you always end up with more pain than you deserve…

We didn't talk much after that. I began walking away from the garden. Part of me was thinking that she would stop me. I was waiting, walking as slowly as I could. She didn't speak a word. Not a single damn word!

I was surrounded completely by emptiness as I walked by the deserted dark lane that connected the gardens and the hostel. After a few moments, I could walk no further. I sat under a nearby tree. My cellphone vibrated. It was her message.

Pls come back. Dnt leave me…

I felt an immediate urge to go back to her. I got up, wiped my wet eyes, and prepared myself to confront her. Although I didn't have the courage to ask her about Vicky, we did need to talk.

I decided to call her. I hit '2' on my speed dial. The call got connected within seconds. One ring, two rings, three… ten rings…

I called her up again, but she didn't receive my call. My phone vibrated for a message again.

Pls 4gt wht I said. Pls come back to me. I wil 4gt abt Vicky...

The conflict between my heart and brain began anew. Should I go back to her? *Maybe she was just too confused about herself,* said my brain. I began walking towards the garden again.

A few moments later she appeared. We glanced at each other for a couple of seconds. Without a word, she rushed into my arms, bursting into an ocean of tears.

"I'm not so selfish Aarav. I love you. I can't destroy your life just for my own happiness"

What did she mean? Was she with me, just because she didn't want to hurt me? Everything was so clear, but my heart would still not believe it.

I couldn't help but smile. It was a fake smile. It was a result of my uncontrollable emotions. I was smiling, just for her sake. Her heart was beating for someone else, but still I was living. There was no hope left. But I was still living, just for her...

DIL, DOSTI, ETC...

"Why don't you just go and sleep with her once," Rony suggested.

"Fuck you Rony...!"

"Not me baby!"

Rony was one spoilt bastard. The only thing that crossed his mind when talking about girls was getting them into bed. He was of the opinion that once you sleep with a girl, she wouldn't leave you, ever. I only marveled about his lack of feelings, and wondered if there was a way I could change his thoughts. He had a thing for Reena, and we all knew about it. He used to be about a hundred kilos before he met Reena, and things suddenly changed. Walking several kilometers every morning, for a couple of months and he was ready to get into bed with Reena; only if she agreed! He came down to sixty-five kilograms only to find Reena was not really interested in him...

He bought a Pulsar 220. She refused to ride on it. He went ahead to buy a lavish Honda City. That changed the whole scenario. But Reena was either too smart, or too disinterested in Rony, or just too dumb. She didn't even bother a bit about Rony... Occasionally, she would come along with a few friends, and ask Rony for a lift to the market. Poor Rony couldn't even flirt with her! Maybe it was after several such episodes that his feelings and love really died away.

Several months passed since then. He smoked heavily these days. Sometimes about ten cigarettes a day, with either *Signature* or *Imperial Blue* every week. He has changed a lot. He still thought about Reena, but not in romantic dreams anymore, just porn!

"I think she loves you, but just needs some more space and time," Bhalu explained.

"I'm sure Einstein would be proud of you Bhalu," said Rony.

Wow...I was lying in misery. I had my fourth breakup. And these lunatics were making fun of it. But wait, they didn't even know that we had just broken up. They didn't know it was the fourth time. So their reactions weren't really bad. All of us had been through love at some point of time in life. But only some people felt the difference that love caused in their whole being.

As Bhalu puts it –

'I had actually stopped watching porn. I didn't fantasize about cozying up with her until the day we broke up.'

That offers a piece of advice, although I might not take it –

Never judge a girl by her looks...

Some friends are real bastards. At times, you felt you shouldn't have been with them. I felt like killing Rony. We even had a few fights. But in the end, either Bhalu or DKP would mend the whole situation. There was something about friends that couldn't be denied – attachment. I couldn't live without my friends, but today I feel this needs a serious re-consideration.

Bhalu said something after which we doubt his mental incapability –

"Never give up, not because you still have tomorrow to try again, but because...you may not have tomorrow to try again."

On second thoughts, the part where he says 'you may not have tomorrow to try again' might actually be more meaningful than he meant it to be.

"You know what? Marriage is a *workshop*, where the man *works*, and the wife *shops*..." explained Bhalu.

"Can you just stuff your ass up your mouth for a while, eh Bhalu?" shouted Rony. I didn't understand why he behaved so badly sometimes.

That night I wrote the following piece, for 'Ishq'...

Of course, I dont miss you... :P

I don't know how and why, but now is the perfect time to start writing this. I don't know why I said so, I don't know even if I mean it, I don't know if I may continue writing this but yes I am writing this at the moment. You know, since you had asked me to be your friend, my mind hasn't been at rest. It just keeps thinking. Sometimes I just feel like shouting to my brain "Shut up!! Stupid, let me sleep," but brain, and that too my stupid brain has now become wild. I mean not that hot, sexy and wild wala wild but domestic and wild animals wala wild. I mean it's not domestic anymore. To be more specific it doesn't listen to me now, it is not under my control. It does what it wants. But why am I writing all this. This account is just to tell that I don't miss you.

Today, after a long time, I actually felt good, met DKP, Bhalu and Rony. We watched DON-2 together. I thought I wouldn't miss u now since I had my friends with me. I saw Priyanka in the movie. She was hot and sexy. Then I thought, 'Oh c'mon! my 'Ishq' is much much beautiful than you (stupid Priyanka). Then I received your text, and I started missing you badly.

I just wanted to talk to you. I wanted to open way2sms right then and reply you but then I thought "Dude, don't miss her and watch the movie ;)"

I tried watching the movie again, tried laughing at the jokes, tried NOT TO MISS YOU but no point trying because even in trying not to miss you, I was missing you. I was missing you badly. But I didn't know why there was something positive about missing you today.

Is it the happiness of meeting friends, or the eagerness to meet you?

But yes, today morning was the same as usual, SLEEPLESS and DISTURBING.

Hanging out with my friends had actually relaxed me, filled me with some kind of positive energy. And at the end of the day, here I was – Happy (don't know why, I'm quite surprised). It's just that I was missing you positively now. It felt like 'yes ma'am, I can wait for you forever.'

Today I have actually missed you more than I should...

Of course I wouldn't miss you tomorrow... :P

Gud night my baby... ;)

5TH AND THE LAST...

I was lying in deep emotional pain, in my room when my phone rang. 'Ishq' flashed on my phone screen after a long time. It had been just three days since she told me she loves Vicky more than me. So I was confused whether I wanted to receive that call or not. But as always, I wasn't brave enough to decline orders of my heart. I answered the call.

"Hi…" she said.

"Hmm…"

"Can you come at the canteen at 2? I want to meet you…"

'I want to meet you'…those words ignited a fresh spark in my heart. Maybe she wanted to apologize for her behavior that day. Maybe she didn't really love Vicky and was a bit confused. Maybe she loved me, after all.

"Yes. Sure." I said. She disconnected the call.

It was half past one, so I got up to get ready.

'Finally, 'Ishq' has realized her mistake' I thought. She wanted to meet me. She wanted to express her true love for me,,,

Again, the eight minute long walk to the canteen felt like the most enriching walk in the campus. I could see the beautiful flowers, shrubs and bushes again. I could feel the happiness in the air. I could feel compassion and love. Everything suddenly began to seem to beautiful...

'Ishq' was waiting for me there. She was holding a bag in her hand.

She looked at me. Although my heart was still in pain, I wanted to live that moment. I wanted to lose myself in 'Ishq', and I wanted to love her.

"Hi..." she said.

She was expressionless.

'Maybe she realized her mistake' I thought again.

"I love you 'Ishq'. I can never live without you. I know even you can't live without me..."

But before I could speak anything more, she pulled out a teddy bear from the bag and kept it on the table nearby. My heart stopped beating.

Then she pulled out several greeting cards, and placed them next to the teddy bear. A tear dropped from my left eye, and then another...

She didn't even look at me while removing her earrings, and kept them on the table. I became unconscious and fell back on the chair next to me. Another tear dropped from my right eye.

Without looking at me, she turned her back towards me and began walking away.

I was devastated, completely. Hurt, deserted, and lost. I sat still at that table for a long time...I looked at that teddy bear which I had gifted her on her birthday. Those cards, which I used to gift her occasionally, were lying there. I had become as useless as those cards. Those earrings, from our first valentine's day together, made me cry insanely.

How many times can you stab a heart with a knife? Or let me put this question in a slightly different manner. How many times would it hurt when you are stabbed again and again with a knife? When does the pain start vanishing? Or does it even stop hurting ever? I know the answer. Do You?

I have been struck five times... and now the pain is finally starting to decrease...somewhat...

I hadn't been talking about a real knife here. I just meant getting hurt in love. It just felt like being stabbed with a knife. And I was stabbed with one such knife last night (9th Dec 2011). Now this reminded me of Decembers, the last month of the year. It was the time when one eagerly waited for the month to end so that a new year could be welcomed. Last year, in December I was feeling extremely sick as Nivedita had broken my heart.

This year, again, I was thinking of putting an end to this suffering of love. There were millions of means hovering around in my head. I just didn't know which one to choose. But all this reminded me of my own personal quotes –

"Never think of dying for those whom you love, think of living for those who love you"

It has been said that the best way to endure the pain caused by love was to convert it into words and this was what I was trying to do. The story that follows is the story of my five break ups or those five times when hundreds of knives stabbed my heart. By now you must realize that I am not a good boy. Having five break-ups clearly spoke of my character. Believe me – I had the same opinion about myself.

Today (10ᵗʰ Dec 2011): I updated my Facebook with 3 posts in the morning at intervals of five minutes each. FB posts, something which I hadn't done in a very long time. The posts were:

1. *"Aise veerane main ek din ghut ke marr jayenge hum, Jitna jee chahe pukaro phir nahi ayenge hum..."*

2. "No matter whether you try or not, sand will slip, right thru your hand"

3. "An original thought: There are 2 reasons for a man to commit suicide – When he is not able to face this race or disgrace"

The first and third might seem quite convincing regarding my issues with life and death but the second one, it had a story behind it.

It all started on 31ˢᵗ Jan 2011, the turning point of my life. It was the day when the most beautiful part of my life, my connection with 'Ishq', began. Truly, she was divine. I had been chatting with 'Ishq' for the last 2 nights. We didn't sleep on the night of 30ᵗʰ Jan and chatted for the whole night and repeated that on 31ˢᵗ.

Something which I hadn't dreamt of was actually happening. A girl, and not just any girl, 'Ishq', whom I really loved from the bottom of my heart was going to be mine. I felt I was at the peak of Mount Everest. She asked me how I would propose, if I were to propose to her. I was shocked to hear this but she said – "C'mon go on, you might not get this chance again" – and without even thinking for a second I forwarded her the poem I had written for her. She was very happy.

"….Now, I have understood that she is like sand. More I would try to hold her, more she would move away, from my hand…So this time, I set her free, If it's is meant to be, She will come back to me…."

The bold lines would very well explain my second FB status. Anyway, I was happy that she was happy; everything was perfect. I managed to get her to explain our relationship on the morning of 30th and she said we were special friends. By the morning of 31st, we were committed to each other. Not special friends, but the 'birds who decided to live in the cage of each other's love *aur jo ab kisi kaam ke nahi reh gaye…*' (The way 'Ishq' described it). I proposed to her again with a poem but a different one.

And everything was perfect! <3

My best buddy, DKP, woke up in the morning and I told him everything. You must have someone with whom you could discuss these matters otherwise things could get troublesome. You always need a so called love guru, a friend who could give you the best advice on love but was, mysteriously, single himself! DKP, however, was a rare guy. He wasn't single, yet a *love-guru*.

They say there is someone's blessing behind every good thing that happens. On 28th January I had met a small boy outside the mall begging for money. And I had one last coin left in my wallet. For some unexplained reason I couldn't refuse the boy and I agreed to give him my last coin only if he would say that '*Ishq tumse pyar karne lagegi aur sirf tumse hi pyar karegi.*' He had said it. My last coin became his at that very moment and 'Ishq' became mine three days later. The boy was unforgettable and I sometimes referred to him as GOD himself who had come there to bless me. And that very evening 'Ishq' commented on her sketch made by me in the class that I had uploaded on FB. She said, "When am I gonna get my sketch artist Aarav," and I could almost feel butterflies in my stomach. I was on cloud number nine. The impossible was happening finally…

SAFEST WAY TO KILL ME...

You don't need a knife, or some bullets
To kill me,
Believe me dear, it is much more easy...
Just act like you care for me,
And I would fall in love with you,
Betray my trust and
That's all –
I'm almost dead...
But don't take a chance!
Act like you are sorry and
Restart the romance...
Betray me again,
Now I stop trusting people and
My heart is dead,
I'm a cripple...
Without my heart,
I'm nothing more than dead.
Your purpose is served!
And for this crime, you
Won't be condemned...

LAST THREE DAYS OF MY LIFE...PART 1

Within 10 days, I had decided to commit suicide but I was still not sure of the method I would be using to end my life. The method which I use should be such that it causes death in a very short time and minimum pain. It should be such that there would practically be no chances of me being saved, under any circumstances, by any blessed doctor on earth. I didn't want to take any chances. I knew it was an irreversible step but I was left with no other option. The possible ways that I have thought of, to end my life are as follows...

Cut my wrists. Possible weapons would be Bhalu's knife (I have heard it slices chicken as if it were butter) or a knife that I'd take from my aunt's house or a paper cutter bought for this very special purpose. Possible places to end my life would be my aunt's place or the hostel's last washroom (the last one only due to the fact that it is not used very often plus it is very clean!). Now in the hostel I had to make sure that I died. I would take at least 5 blood thinners which are actually pain killers. In fact, fortunately or unfortunately, Disprin turns out to be one great blood thinner. It means blood from my wounds would not clot and there would be continuous blood loss. I would need at least 8-10 hours alone after I cut my wrists. This would ensure that most of the blood drains out. The only disadvantage with this method was that I MAY SURVIVE. Actually, I analysed the after effects of the situation in which I might survive: I would be lying on a hospital bed on life support system. 'Ishq' would come back to me and confess her love for me – I would be expelled from IIT due to such an attempt – I would feel like a loser for the rest of my life – my family would hate me – I would sit in some retail shop for the rest of my life – Finally, I would never get married to 'Ishq', as that happens only in fairy tales. The risks were high in this method, and also the pain. I was not sure if I would be able to bear the pain due to a cut in my wrist for several hours without letting anyone know about it.

Hang from a ceiling fan. The most common one. So common that, I was actually tempted to call it the 'traditional' way of ending one's miseries once and for all. I hadn't been able to figure out how I would be able to do that because I had no prior experience of this method (not that I had prior experience of cutting wrists, just that there was not much scientific explanation available for this method). For this I had to get my window fixed, which could be opened by anyone from outside as of now, so that it could not be opened by any means; because this might result in failure of my suicide and it would turn into just another suicide attempt making my life worse than hell just like a failed attempt of cutting wrists would. Not to mention too much money wasted in getting a good quality rope or something. What would I tell the shopkeeper? "*Bhaiya*, give me a rope long and strong enough to let me hang from the ceiling fan for about ten minutes..." Crap! It would take some time before I could make up my mind. Also, I needed to get my chair out of Bhalu's room. Yes, Bhalu had two chairs that belonged to me. I needed them before I could think of executing this plan. The advantage of this method was that it was short, simple, sweet and painless (I mean less painful). It would just take three minutes to execute and I would be done with it. No sufferings, nothing. Or this one again, I could execute at my aunt's place as it would be vacant for the next ten days as she had planned to go to Delhi.

Jumping off the fort. The fort was just a few kilometres from the IIT campus, so it would be a very convenient option. Or for that matter, even Himalayas, or any other place very high above sea level would do. It would actually be fun because I had always wanted to try some adventure sport and a fort has those heights. Besides, I had read that I would die even before I touch the ground due to heart attack so that would be less painful, I guess. It was somewhat like experiencing the best joys just before dying. Another advantage was that there were absolutely no chances of survival. I had never heard someone surviving a 500-feet fall. People die after falling from a 4-storey, in movies; could I survive after falling from about 40 storeys? Not very difficult to say. And yes, the best part was that I could make it look completely like an accident (I could ask my friends to take a pic or something and then I would act like I slipped...Ooops...my mistake). This had its own benefits. Many onlookers would have their first experience of seeing a person falling from a hill. Many lovers would never ever try to make love stories on that fort (No, seriously, because love is painful in the end). Also, this method clears all complications, so that 'Ishq' had no regrets on the part that I died because of her. And, my people won't curse 'Ishq' now and then for my death. I must make sure 'Ishq' continues her life as normally as possible. I wanted to die, but I didn't want to make her life uncomfortable and regretful.

Those were the 3 possible ways in which I was going to end my life. The best one was jumping off the fort, but I didn't know if I had enough strength for it. The easiest one was the second one but I didn't know if I would be able to execute it or not. The first one was worth exploring and I was more inclined towards it. There was too much confusion. I needed an approach that was streamlined for me. And finally, that will depend on the situation and the timing, on the day this would happen…

Now, that was all about the ways of committing suicide. The next question was finding the perfect date. Which date, must I choose to die on..? I had decided upon some criteria for choosing the date. I shall have to avoid some of the dates…

It should be a date which is already associated with me so that it doesn't give people one more day to be sad for me. For e.g. it could be my birthday. So that people don't have two different days to be sad, i.e., my birthday and my death day. Instead they would remain sad for only one day. Another one would be 31st January, my commitment date with 'Ishq'. This date would remind 'Ishq' of me always so she would be sad after I am gone. I was not sure if I wanted her to be sad, but somewhere, deep inside my heart, I had this desire to let her remember throughout her life how much she meant to me.

Any date but 31ˢᵗ Jan because if I died on 31ˢᵗ, 'Ishq' would feel like I died for her. It was all because of her and this wouldn't let my soul be at peace. Although that would be perfectly true, I would not really want this to happen.

And I just can't take this pain any more so the date should be as soon as possible.

Now, the most appropriate date that I could think of as the best one is 1ˢᵗ Feb.

It is possible that 'Ishq' would realize things on her own and comes back to me on 31ˢᵗ, our commitment date. Even this happened only in movies, but I expected at least one per cent similarity between movies and factual happenings. So, there happened to be some chance.

I didn't suffer the agony of failing minor exams to be held from 6ᵗʰ – 8ᵗʰ Feb. Although I hadn't studied anything I could surely get enough marks, but given the mental condition I was in, it might not be possible.

Now that the date of suicide was fixed, another question was that of a suicide note. There had to be a suicide note. And this note had to be such that it reduces everyone's grief over my death. Some people would be much more concerned with my suicide than the others and I needed to mention them here –

Mom, my sweet mom. I would be really sorry to die because before I truly fell in love with 'Ishq', I wanted to do everything for her. She was my goddess. I wanted to make her happy throughout her life. It's not that I didn't want to make her happy now. I still wanted to do everything I could to make her happy but there was this pain inside me that was not letting me live. It was a pain that refused to go. This pain of betrayal or being left alone or whatever it was left me completely fed up. It had already been more than a month since we had broken up and I was shattered. Millions of pieces of my heart, which could never be put together, were giving me an excruciating pain which increased with every passing moment and would finally kill me. Very soon.

Sunny bro, my brother. I always loved and respected him very much. Always wanted to be like him. He was just so much dedicated to mom and dad. And that's what made me jealous of him. OOOOH!! He had always been a star. His AIEEE rank had been far better than mine. His State Entrance Exam rank had also been better than mine. He had been sporty while I was completely dumb. He would really be angry with me for all this because he just couldn't see mom sad. One pandit had once predicted that my bro would be like Shravan kumar. He would serve mom and dad. I just couldn't live with this pain in my heart. My departure will definitely increase pressure over him and shatter my family's desires; but, as I said, I couldn't live with this pain in my heart.

Dad, the most complicated figure in the mind of any son. I always had mixed feelings for my dad. There were times when I felt so much love for him and there were times when I hated him the most. I knew he had done so much for me. He worked day and night to earn for my studies, to make our lives better and comfortable but then, he had done some bad things, which I hated him for. He's dominating, and possessive. Although I felt I had inherited some of his possessiveness which would increase with time, I think he could have been better. Wait, my possessiveness couldn't increase, because I didn't have much time left. Whatever it was, being my dad he deserved a suicide note.

Suchita and Dhirendra Kapur aka suchi & DKP. My besties. They had done so much for me or maybe I felt that way. Though, *agar dekha jaye toh maine bhi kucch kum toh nahi kia unke liye* but that's a part of life. A friend in need is always a friend, indeed. I helped Suchi and DKP whenever they needed me. There were been times, they explained certain things to that nobody else could, just like five days ago, when I had not been eating for 3 days continuously –

Day 1: Lassi (to block my throat), one cheese sandwich (I couldn't control when I saw my friends having one), one cigarette (which Rony got me dunno from where)…

Day 2: *Meethi imli* (as I was reminded of my early school days when I was in 1st, when my school ended I used to eat it), one cheese sandwich (curse you, DKP, for intentionally savouring that delicious sandwich in front of me and mocking me)

Day 3: Two *paranthas* with which I ended my fast

It was all because of bloody DKP, that I had to end my fast-unto-death plan. He called Suchi and 'Ishq' after our 6 – 8 pm .NET classes and all three of them – Suchi, DKP and 'Ishq' took turns to scold me. All of them were trying to blackmail me emotionally. I resisted as much as I could but finally 'Ishq' *ke aansuo ne tod dia mujhe* and I ended up being played with again, by 'Ishq'.

'Ishq' did that every time – Emotional blackmail is the word for it. I just felt like I had made up a dog of myself, a pet dog who wears a tag indicating its belonging to 'Ishq'. I wasn't like that earlier. There were times when I controlled her. There were times when I controlled myself, my feelings. Now, what I would call myself is an 'Out of control DOG'... I was in deep shit and the song *'Ban gaya kutta...'* played in an infinite loop in my head...

> *"Bandh gaya patta, Dekho ban gaya Kutta...Baandh '*
> *ishq' ka patta, Dekho ban gaya kutta..."*

Anyway let's continue with Suchi and DKP and talk about 'Ishq' later. So, it was due to their initiative that I lived to write this account. And yes, Suchi had been my crush at some point of time in life and I had feelings for her but that was something different from love (so DKP, dude if you are reading this, you can be assured that I have never betrayed you). Maybe, it was true friendship that I always felt for her. And DKP had always been so kind to give me his shoulder to cry on; and of course his t-shirts to spoil with my runny nose! Also, he had been hearing of my pain continuously for days and weeks. So, they both deserved a suicide note.

F4 and my old friends. We had a *fabulous* group of four guys, that's where F4 comes from. I would like to specially mention Bhalu, who had been my roomie for the maximum period. Though it was I, who had hijacked his room since 2nd semester; DKP was my first buddy in college and his room was right next to mine. As a matter of fact it still is right next to mine even after we have shifted to a different hostel. Bhalu had always been a caring brother. He was one of the most extremist guys I had ever seen. He was always on extremes of sadness, anger, happiness, or whatever feelings he was able to express. He was a hyper. That's what I loved about him. Then there is Rony, *jhaantu hai saala. Usko samjhna* impossible *hai.* I never understood what he wanted from life. He once told me, "I have always looked upon you as my younger brother". *Shayad bakchodi kar raha tha.* I don't know whether he meant it or not but yes, I somehow began feeling like his younger brother since then. Together, we used to have a lot of fun. We were like anti-girl guys. We used to play pranks on girls and spoil their excessive make-up with water sprinklers. We used to comment on how bad they were looking or how their boyfriends were gay, and many other things. Amitav Sridhar, aka Amit, I could never make out whether he was a friend or not but at times when I needed him, he was always there and when he needed me I was always there. Our friendship became more formal after I joined IIT and he joined some local engineering college. We just help each other out. I didn't remember getting emotional with him or vice versa and if I did, he would make fun of my feelings. He was a retarded motherfucker but yes he had a place in my heart.

Mr. Motherfuckerguitarist, sorry…Mr. MFG. I called Vicky by this name from the day I discovered his affair with 'Ishq'. He had ruined my life and so he deserved it. So Mr.

MFG, Nivedita Raj and Aarav Virani, would be the three people responsible for my death. Nivedita was my first ever best friend who was a girl. I met her in IIT and eventually got attracted to her, began experiencing feelings for her. I used to share almost everything with her. Another reason for this attraction was the fact that Nivedita-Suchi were besties, me-DKP were besties, DKP-Suchi loved each other, me-Nivedita made some sense so I ended up proposing to her and got a 'NO' in reply because she was already committed to another idiot influenced by her aura. It was later, that I found 'Ishq' and fell in love with her. And kept thinking now and then how I could even like Nivedita, she looked ugly! I think I was lucky that she refused to accept my love as I found 'Ishq' later on. But, whatever it was, I was left heartbroken after I was rejected.

Then, it took me some time to get better.

Now, how would Nivedita be responsible for my death? Simple, because had she accepted my proposal at that time, I wouldn't have met 'Ishq' and would probably have been happy now. So you, who are reading this, would never have been reading this. So you must thank Nivedita while I curse her. Curse her for accepting that Sri Lankan *firangi* as her boyfriend. And about Mr. MFG, I would be talking later on in this. And Mr. Aarav Virani would be a mystery.

Masi's house. I have had some really good moments at this place, spent almost half of my life here. My sisters over here love me. Then, there was Masi, who had seen me growing up. Then, Mausaji, I had always wanted to be like him. At times,

I hated my Mausaji too but yes I loved and respected him a lot as well.

That's all for the suicide note thing and sorry if I missed anyone. Oooops!! I think I missed one name. Can you guess the name...? Of course – the one and only – 'Ishq'. But did she really deserve a note? If I forgot to mention it later on, it would mean I didn't consider it worthwhile. Now, I have to decide one last wish for myself and some last things that I want to do. Here, I have a list of things I would have to do before I leave the world:

- ✓ Schedule texts and mails for 30 days for Suchi, 'Ishq', DKP, and bro...

- ✓ Return 'Ishq' her gifts and letters, just like she did. But I had not decided whether to keep a pic of them or not.

- ✓ For 'Ishq', I had either to make her my bestest friend, or make myself hate her (second one is difficult to choose)

- ✓ Delete every sign of 'Ishq' associated with me. I would format my lappy, FB messages and mails...and I'll mail the folder to DKP/Suchi before dying...

- ✓ And yes, delete every message from my phone after typing them out in my lappy.

- ✓ Clear all debts.

By now, you would be convinced that I was extremely mentally sick. I took three of my break ups with sanity but since the fourth one I began to lose sanity and now I felt I was schizophrenic after my fifth and last break up. I was going to end my suffering once and for all now. I was going to end my life.

I also knew that somewhere, somehow, it was I who was responsible for my pain. *Main bhi koi doodh ka dhula hua nahi hun* and maybe I deserved it. Anyway recently I had been reflecting –When was the perfect time for a person to die..? I could answer it thus –

When there were more people who would bless you for your death, who would benefit from your death or who would be happy to see you dead.

When your loved ones hate you, it was time to go.

Both these reasons suited well to me.

Regrets, regrets, regrets. Oh God!! Why did you make them? They will kill me.

Another shock came straight to me. He told he saw 'Ishq' with Mr. MFG and both of them were talking and blushing.

I thought I made fun of myself by staying even after that but. I must go. My presence couldn't make 'Ishq' return, so maybe my absence could do that for me. I think that's where I would stop writing about 'Day 1'. So that is all for today. I am exhausted. I would watch 18th annual screen awards now. Enough of Ishq done, now time for some entertainment...

LAST THREE DAYS OF MY LIFE...PART 2

Last night, I kept thinking – I was finally becoming optimistic. Time heals everything. The boy who was so negative as to commit suicide for a girl he had known since one and a half year was slowly turning optimistic. Time for laughs and mockery for you (whoever you are reading this). Now, let me come to the point. I was thinking of several things, which are...

Why does 'Ishq' ask me to leave so early even when we meet after long durations..?

The pessimist in me puts it this way –

Is that because she hated me..? Is that because she found me boring..?

The new born optimist in me argues –

Is that because she was afraid of falling for me again if I was with her continuously..? Was it because the more she saw me, the more she had a pain inside her that reminded her of her betrayal..? Is it because she still loved me..?

I had already thought for more than a month. Now it was time to listen to the optimistic me. The optimist decided to hack DKP's account. Now, where did DKP come from all of a sudden? And why would I hack DKP's account when I had to know about 'Ishq'..? This is because there had been something fishy about him lately. I had been feeling that he didn't tell me some things. He cursed 'Ishq' on my face but he had been chatting secretly with 'Ishq' for quite some time. The events that led me to this conclusion were:

1. A month ago, when I used to cry to DKP on Gtalk, sometimes he just went crazy and filled me continuously with the crap that Mr. MFG and 'Ishq' were online and there was something going on between them, and that 'Ishq' was not a good girl and I must leave her.

2. A few days ago, when I had been hungry for 3 days, he had told me, "Dude, don't feel like you are the only one suffering here, 'Ishq' has also been crying for 3 days, and she too is suffering without you." Now the question is – how the hell would he know about that?

3. I remembered him saying once, "*Yaar, mujhe toh nahi lagta ki* she has got anything to do with Mr. MFG. She is just using his name to create distances from you. Maybe she still loves you madly."

4. Yesterday, he just kept saying that he had seen 'Ishq' and Mr. MFG together thrice in a couple of days. I didn't know if that was possible but I didn't want to believe it until I saw it with my own eyes.

To conclude, I felt there was something strange about DKP. I felt DKP and 'Ishq' had decided that they will continuously make me feel that there was something between her and Mr. MFG, and that was their plan of creating distances between me and 'Ishq' and making me hate her. We would see what DKP's Gmail had to say. I just couldn't wait to open it to have some secrets revealed. I would be able to do that only the next time I was in the hostel, so I would try to make it to the hostel today or tomorrow. I need to clear these doubts and get my answers.

The time was about 7:20 pm. I had tried to hack DKP's Gmail account but couldn't. I felt quite frustrated. I couldn't ask someone else to do it, as I didn't want anyone to know what I was up to. This mystery was killing me. What was it that 'Ishq' really wanted? I thought DKP had sided with her. But he sure had some plans; after all, he was my closest friend. I was sure he wouldn't be up to something I didn't particularly like. I was very very angry at the moment. I just felt like bashing someone up. Poor me, I couldn't even do that, given my limited physical capabilities.

THE REENA ISSUE

Now, let me tell you about the matter with Reena. Let's get back to my three day hunger strike once again. I was already damn angry by the time I returned from the Girl's hostel where Suchi, DKP and 'Ishq' convinced me to have some food. We ordered *paranthas*. I ate two, give or take a half. Now, my anger was directed towards girls. I was damn angry with girls on the whole. The First thing I did was calling Chandni (bhalu's ex-girlfriend) and cursing and scolding her badly for betraying my friend. Then, it was time for some chatting on Gtalk. I opened my Gtalk and there were three girls online: Reena (a group mate of 'Ishq' and a close friend of hers), Deepika, and Prachi (another friend of 'Ishq'). Bad luck, girls! I began with Reena. I started making indirect comments about her and she got angry. She said "I know how shallow you are…" and the words were just unbearable for me. I just couldn't control myself and said things I shouldn't have said, in anger. I was fighting and cursing girls, and felt awesome when my friends said 'it feels like the old Aarav is back' and I thought like I was getting all better.

But it wasn't like that. In fact I was getting worse this time.

I just couldn't forgive myself for talking to Reena like that. Since then, I apologized several thousand times to myself but to no avail. I couldn't gather enough courage to say 'sorry' to her and last evening when I was talking to 'Ishq', I made her feel like I still didn't care about the Reena issue at all. But I couldn't control that as well. I called 'Ishq' and told her how sorry I was and I would say the same to Reena, whenever I could gather enough courage.

FRUSTRATED LOVER...

The semester results brought about a change in how people around me perceived me. My Cumulative Grade Point Average (CGPA) was 9.6 with the GPA for that semester being a perfect 10. Instantly I became popular on the campus as 'the guy who manages both grades and a girlfriend efficiently'. I became so popular among the fresher's batch that some people would actually ask me for tips as to how they could best manage their girlfriend along with studies.

"The key thing to note is that even she is a student, just like you," I explained to the young guy.

"But my girlfriend is doing a Bachelor in Mass Media... I mean, she doesn't have to study. She keeps pestering me that I don't spare enough time for her..."

What was I? A love-guru or something?

"See, I managed it in the college setup. If you want to do it like I did, first get a girlfriend on the same campus!"

Needless to say, neither he nor anybody else ever came to me asking for advice on love after that...

To tell the truth, I was having a mad time managing my

love life, and it wasn't actually love by now. It was more of a compulsion for her...

When something is wrong between you and your girlfriend, on a campus like this one, almost everyone comes to know about it. And that only increases the suffering associated with it.

Now the fact that my CGPA was 9.6 didn't help ease my situation. In fact, it made me feel worse. I surely had a bright future with that score, and I was a good lover too. But why did 'Ishq' still consider Mr. MFG as a better option? What did he do? He fucking played a guitar? Where would he play a guitar? In bars, no...trains, no...on the streets? That only meant I was a loser in spite of having a 9.6?!! That street guitar player didn't study, played a fucking guitar and took my girl? This was seriously frustrating. I mean, I felt that being a topper had made me automatically attractive to geeky girls. Girls usually love guys who are popular among other girls. But 'Ishq'... she had ditched me for that stupid guitarist? I was a loser. A fucking geek loser. I had put all my efforts in studies so that we, I and 'Ishq', could have a bright future together. But she had ruined it all. She had ruined everything...

THE BREAKUP PARTY

"They've done it in movies man, C'mon! Be a man!" Rony shouted.

I had broken up the fifth time and these bastards wanted a party. Their idea was actually a noble one. They felt that it might actually help to strengthen my relationship with 'Ishq'. Frankly speaking, they had never been more wrong. There is an awful lot of difference between how things happened in movies and in reality. But Rony and Bhalu were two such people whose brains were so pre-occupied by their own thoughts that they failed to understand anything else.

So they finally convinced me for a breakup party in a five star hotel. All four of us were to have a lavish dinner at the best hotel in town. I distinctly remember the date – 1st February 2012. The date was unforgettable. One year ago, it was the same day when I felt I was the happiest person on earth. It was the day my association with 'Ishq' had begun, and it was the day when it would formally end. That this day was going to form an important aspect of my life, was still largely unknown to me.

At about five in the evening, we had fruit juice at the institute juice center. Everyone was making fun of me and my relationship with 'Ishq'. I was sitting quietly. Rony cracked a lame joke that depressed me. They kept cracking dirty jokes some of which made absolutely no sense.

I didn't say a word. I was sad for several things. Firstly, I had not been able to execute my suicide plan, for which today was the last day. I had missed the deadline. Secondly, I hated any discussion about 'Ishq'. F4 guys knew nothing about me and 'Ishq' and so they felt that it was our first breakup. Only DKP knew that it was our fifth and last one...

Soon, we all came back to the hostel to get ready to go for the party.

"Listen guys. The most important thing to do today is to keep no money with you at all. No money. Except for Aarav, perhaps," said Bhalu. These guys wanted me to become bankrupt before I died. Fine!

At about six in the evening, we booked a cab for 'South Park'. It was the only five-star hotel in this area. I was prepared to shell out a few thousand bucks today, the last few thousand bucks I had.

At the restaurant, there were discussions on various topics ranging from Nived to Suchi to 'Ishq', and every other girl related to any one of us. Bhalu got serious about Chandni, who had dumped him. At least he was true enough to accept that she had dumped him. DKP had also had breakups, but his was a more personal affair as his last breakup was not really the final one. So DKP was only partly in my situation. The reason he was able to manage things so nicely was because he had another, equally cute and loving, girlfriend in his hometown, probably unknown to Suchi. And however strong my friendship with Suchi became, it would never surpass the level of friendship between DKP and me. For such a simply complicated reason, DKP was still enjoying his love life.

I tried to concentrate on the delicious Italian pasta they had served. Italian pasta reminded me of the times 'Ishq' and I had spent in the Italian gardens. We had our first kiss there... it was magical.

She was sitting shyly besides me. It was the same month, the month of February. There was no one around. It was a dark, quiet, cold and romantic evening. I put my left hand around her right hand. She blushed. Slowly I moved closer, and my hand now went round her waist. In reciprocation, she put her right hand around my shoulder. It was the perfect physical setting possible. We kept staring each into other's eyes for about a minute. My heartbeat was rising with every passing second. Soon I could feel her breath, and slowly she closed her eyes. It was an indication from her that I could indeed move ahead. Without wasting any more time, I eliminated that one inch difference which was remaining between our lips, and my lips touched hers. An electric sensation ran down all through my body. I couldn't stop my right hand move up and feel her cheeks. I kissed her again, this time I was more aware of the feeling. She opened her eyes briefly, and moved her left hand to rest it on my face, and we kissed again. This time it was a deep one, lasting longer. The next followed... and then another... and another... My hand was now slowly moving downwards from her face to find a resting place at something softer. During the next kiss, she completely motioned herself in front of me, holding my head in both her hands and kissed me sensuously. My hand was now slowly caressing her soft, round curves, and she was enjoying it comfortably. We kissed furiously for some time.

Suddenly she realized where my hand was, and she used her left hand to move it away slowly, while moving away from the kissing encounter. I observed her as she shyly looked away, smiling and blushing all the way. She adjusted her top, flicked her hair off her shoulders, just as most other beauty-conscious girls with a boyfriend would do. She was looking beautiful. Extremely beautiful. I was lost in a dream again, after a long time. It was the effect of her dreamy eyes. Eyes that would leave their impact on my heart and mind forever...

"Aarav! When did you start taking booze?" Bhalu said as the rest of the guys laughed uncontrollably. They were probably drunk by this time. I looked at the glass in my hand. It didn't look different from water. It was transparent. I took a small sip from the glass. It tasted bitter. Those assholes had put vodka in my glass, probably when I was lost, dreaming about 'Ishq'. I puked the liquid. It tasted disgusting...

"Don't worry dude, you have drunk about 50 ml of that thing already. Where's your mind? Still thinking about Kaavya?" said Bhalu. He was trying to console me but it wasn't easy.

What...the...hell! I was drunk.

"Guys, let's go. I'm feeling uncomfortable here," I told them.

"Sure, just a few more drinks," Rony said.

At about ten in the night, we reached back at the hostel. Everyone was intoxicated, including me.

I was out of control by eleven. I began saying things that I would regret deeply later.

"You know what Rony, maybe I should've actually fucked her."

That caught the attention of everyone in the room. Even Bhalu stopped drinking beer, and began to listen to me.

"And that Motherfuckerguitarist deserves to be fucked…"

"Are you talking about Vicky…Are you fucking talking about Vicky?" Bhalu got enraged, "What has he done? Did he take Kaavya away from you?"

Bhalu came near me. He was facing an emotional trauma now. Bhalu was the kind of person who would do anything for his friends. That Vicky had a lot to do with my breakup was something he would never tolerate.

Seeing no response from me, his eyes became red with anger. I narrated some part of the story to them. How Vicky had come in between me and 'Ishq' and how she loved him more than me.

"I will fucking kill that bastard," he shouted as he left the room.

Rony and I followed him, right up to Vicky's room. He entered straight into Vicky's room and shouted.

"Asshole, motherfucker! I will bash you," said Bhalu as he pushed Vicky hard against the wall. Droplets of blood began dripping from his forehead and lips. He closed his eyes and moaned in pain.

Some other guys came out from their rooms to see what was going on. By this time, Vicky was badly hit and bleeding profusely. I didn't reach out to help Vicky, nor did Rony.

Bhalu was satisfied. He shouted out some more curses before coming back to us.

"You OK now?" he asked me.

"Seriously, like never before!" I was happy. Moreover, I was drunk. And people speak the truth when drunk.

Just then my phone rang. It was a call from Dad.

"Hi Dad!! I'm fine dad! I just fucked that bastard dad..."

I don't remember what else I spoke to Dad. I think I even said a bit about 'Ishq'. Dad could make out the whole situation from just that small conversation I had with him, and with that I destroyed my relations with Dad too. He disconnected the call. It was only later that I realized what a big blunder I had done. I tried to hide this from my F4 guys...

We came back to our rooms and Bhalu began narrating the whole incident to everyone.

"...and then I fucked that moron. I fucked the damn shit out of him. Bloody guitarist..."

Somehow I was feeling good. "You know what guys, this stupid Rony told me Kaavya was the perfect girl for me," I said, feeling dizzy.

"Fucking liar!" shouted Rony.

"Dude, what if you die during your sleep? Won't it be weird...?" This was completely out of context, but I didn't realize it.

"If I die during sleep, I can actually say that I died doing what I love," said Bhalu. We all giggled.

"Bastard, didn't you say, *eleven will be good for you*?" I was back on track.

"What? He gave me the same numerology crap some time back." Bhalu suddenly became alert.

"That! That was utter crap...my buoy!" Rony laughed hard.

This was again something I hated about friends. He had lied to both me and Bhalu that he was an amateur numerologist or something. I believed him, and thought 'Ishq' was the perfect girl for me. I wanted to kill Rony, albeit not literally.

"So you deserve a perfect GPL my buoy..." Bhalu said, with an added emphasis on '*my buoy*', inspired from ZNMD.

"Yesss! Lift this ass," DKP declared. He was always in the mood for fun, even if that meant hurting someone. But today, I actually liked whatever he was doing. What he did to Vicky was not only inhuman, it was *adorable*. It was something I should have done myself, with my own hands.

Rony received a nice beating on his 'G' in the form of G P L.

"C'mon my pussy, now tell us about your darling Reena, will you?" Bhalu was now trying to get on Rony's nerves.

"Yeah baby, she has nice boobies!" said Rony. He was madly intoxicated.

All of us were very much under the effect of alcohol.

I was happy. Alcohol had numbed my senses, and my pain was significantly reduced. It was making me feel a lot better. The breakup party indeed improved my life. For a few hours, although. I would die anyway, I was determined. Nothing could stop me...

UNTOLD AND UNSAID

Things I wanted to say but couldn't tell you...'Ishq'...

I had once very badly hurt my palm. I told you that a lock fell on my palm. That was not the truth. On the previous day, you were angry with me. I went to Mc. Donald's without telling you and you kept waiting for me. You were sad and angry with me and you couldn't talk to me at that moment. I was very sad about hurting you. I tried to convince you that I was sorry but couldn't. You were angry but you never said anything about it. I even tried to convince you with a poem of mine from Suchi's cellphone. I bent down on my knees and recited the poem for you but it didn't work. Though you started speaking to me a bit but I knew you were sad. I just couldn't bear the pain of having to hurt you. I went back to the hostel in DKP's room, shouted as loud as I could. And then started punching my hand against the wall repeatedly until it started bleeding and finally there was a splash of blood on the wall. I tried to sleep but couldn't. For the next eight days, my knuckles hurt badly and I couldn't use my forearm much.

There was a gold coin of two grams that my nephew Chhavi had given me. I had kept it as a lucky charm in my wallet. I never gave it to anybody. Suddenly I told you that I had lost it, one day. I lied. It wasn't lost. You remember Suchi and DKP's commitment party at Royal Palace, when you lied to me and said

"Aarav, my family has decided to get me married to a guy from Canada. I'll have to leave you."

You were obviously kidding but I was gloomy throughout. When we were going to the party you had called me earlier to meet me. You said,

"Today I'm getting dressed up, for you, for the last time…"

…and I was sad thinking 'How can you leave me so soon? I haven't yet understood the meaning of love…'

I was sad througout the party. There were some amazing Ghazal singers who understood the mood very well. We sat hand in hand and I felt it was the last time. I ate with one hand. Well, actually, I ate with two hands but the other one was yours. When we were coming back from the hotel you had a bad bout of coughing. It was uncontrollable. You wanted water. I went to ask for water at a shop but when I checked my wallet I had just that one lucky coin from Chhavi. I called DKP to ask if he had any money. Unfortunately, he didn't and you wanted water badly. I bought water with that coin. I had to convince the shopkeeper that it was indeed gold. But I wasn't sad. Why? Because…

"It was YOU who were my lucky charm not that coin…"

You remember our 8th monthly anniversary of commitment, when you called me in the afternoon to meet me. You were wearing the beautiful white and blue suit that day especially to show me. It was the suit that you probably bought in summer. Suchi came to drop you out of the hostel. There is one thing I never told you that I could never forget those striking looks of yours. There was so much innocence in those looks...

I thought you were 'the cutest girl in the world'. I wanted to tell you that I wanted to see you once again in those looks. I couldn't forget that you had dressed up so beautifully, solely particularly for me. It was one of the cutest things you ever did for me. You might be shocked to hear this but yes I am madly in love with those looks of yours. I love you for it. Thanks for doing it for me.

You remember our fourth break up during the Diwali holidays last year? I just never told you how much pain I was in. I knew that you were in so much pain already and didn't feel like telling you about mine. But for the first time I decided to tell you how much I was hurt, how much pain I was in. So I typed a message but could never gather enough courage to send it to you. The message was...

"You have no idea how much pain I am in. I am going through hell. Every moment that passes sees me wishing only death for myself. I want to die. I haven't slept for a long. I sleep for a short time and then suddenly wake up, thinking about you. My mind couldn't rest. It remains flooded with millions of thoughts, just of you. I couldn't eat a single thing. I felt like vomiting every second. My life was completely screwed up. There was nothing I could do. I could think of nothing but you. I kept checking my mobile phone every couple of minutes. I just couldn't take this hell anymore. I switched off my phone for some time. I didn't know when I would switch it on…"

I never told you, but, yes, you are selfish. You kept saying, "Aarav, I am so selfish. I know this"

But I always used to say, "No, you are not…"

But in my mind, somewhere, I knew that you were indeed selfish. In fact, a very selfish girl, so much so that I hadn't seen a girl as selfish as you were in my entire lifetime. You never cared to think about my feelings, about how I would feel, about how much it would hurt me. You did what you wanted to – always. I wondered whether you thought twice before doing anything.

You remember when Suchi had lost my poems. I was very sad that day. It was maybe 7th or 8th June. You were not there with me, which was the time when we had our first break up. I thought I had lost 2 of the loveliest things in my life – those that I loved too much. Now there were two lies behind that incident.

One, when Suchi told me that she had lost my poems and that she was sorry. I actually felt like shouting at her, scolding her for losing them. They were about 80 of them. I knew I could never re-write them, never ever in my entire life. I felt I would never ever talk to her again and decided never to text her. But then, my heart had to melt and I told her, "no probs, *yaar...* I will rewrite them...no worries, it's just a matter of a few poems."

But it was just not possible not to worry. Those poems were some of the finest things I had done.

Moreover, what she had lost was my love. How would I not be angry? But den after a few days when she texted me, I thought it would be absolutely stupid to lose a good friend in memory of my love. I replied to her, keeping my true feelings hidden. But there was anger inside me, which got suppressed with time.

Secondly I didn't tell you about losing the poems. I thought this might make you think that I'm very much hurt and that would bother you. And at that time and you would patch up with me although I never wanted you to patch up with me because of sympathy. But when we returned from holidays, I told you about losing those poems and that I was very sad after losing poems and it had hurt me much more than losing you. You know something? I had lied. It was the break-up that had hurt me the most and was making me depressed. Losing the poems was hurtful but the pain of losing you was beyond this universe.

The funniest part is that you said, "You could have even lied about it, that missing me hurt you more," and I was thinking in my mind, "I have indeed lied my darling!"

You are a big liar, promise-breaker, and what not. We never broke up on phone, as you would often tell Suchi.

When we patched up after our third break up, you pointed

out the problems you had with me. You pointed out my mistakes – at least then you should have enjoyed being with me after the so called 'long time'. It somehow hurt me. A lot.

I changed completely, only to find that you had left me.

I told you I was weak. There was no one I was attached to, except you. But you didn't understand me, never took me seriously.

When you were going home in summers – our last day together – the morning, you remember you asked me never to leave you and I promised I would never leave you no matter what happened.

You were my weakness or my strength?

I would feel jealous when you told about your crushes to me.

Girls just don't have a heart. They don't know how to love.

I can't die, as you will regret. Actually, when I die, it means I have stopped caring for your feelings, so don't regret my death.

THE LAST THREE DAYS, PART 3

Dad disowned me. He said I was not his son because he hadn't expected me to take alcohol and talk like that. He even came to know about 'Ishq' a bit, and said I must never show him my face. I have lost another reason to live. That's enough. I have already missed two important deadlines – today, and yesterday. Tomorrow, just a few hours from now, would be the ultimate destiny of Aarav Virani…

A little past midnight…I became more and more firm about my last decision. I came out from my room to go to the toilet. I saw Rony walking up and down in the corridor.

"What's up?" He asked me.

"Nothing…what are you up to?"

"I am thinking of going on a long adventurous bike ride…"

He usually did such insane things, so I wasn't amazed. In fact, I was angry at him because he had helped 'Ishq' and Vicky to come together. Suddenly something came to my mind and I said,

"Dude, I need to study. And you see these guys are always disturbing."

"Yeah man…so, what do you want me to do?"

"I want you to lock my door from outside and pass me the keys through the ventilator. Will you do that for me?"

"Sure man. But it's funny that you want to get your room locked!" said Rony. I ignored him.

He locked my room, and threw the keys through the ventilator above the door and left. 3rd February 2012. I was in my room, locked from outside. I was fighting with myself over the issue – whether to commit suicide or not. I was thinking of hanging from the ceiling fan. I chose nicotine poisoning to end my life but it didn't seem to be a good method. I read on internet that it took 30-40 cigarettes to kill a person but I couldn't smoke more than 3 cigarettes out of 33 cigarettes that I had bought yesterday. I couldn't rest. I didn't have breakfast or lunch in the day. I was lying idle in the room, unsure of my next step.

I decided to end my life by hanging. Sorry everyone…

But before that I would have one last conversation with Vicky. I wanted to know if he would keep 'Ishq' happy, after all.

Mustering lot of courage, I opened my laptop to chat with Vicky. He had wanted to tell me something about 'Ishq' earlier, so maybe now I could listen to what he wanted to say…

3:03 PM

I: *der..?*

Vicky: *yup…*

I: Say what you wanted to say...

Vicky: *Nothing, just wanted to ask what you want for her now*

I: Happiness...in any way. How is that possible?

I didn't expect any answer from him. He didn't care to answer either.

3:06 PM

I: Dude...

He didn't reply...

3:07 PM

I: der..?

Vicky: *You have been with her more, so you know her better...*

3:10 PM

I: But never let her become weak because of yourself. I hope you understood what I am trying to say.

Again there was no reply...After some time, I wrote further –

3:13 PM

I: I am quite weak myself. Very weak...Maybe you would understand that someday, surely...

Vicky: *I had understood everything a year ago.*

I: A year ago?

Vicky: *Yes, right after our fresher's party. At that time, I had done what was good for both of you.*

I was shocked. What was he talking about? Was he trying to say that he sacrificed his love for me?

I: Just answer one question, you don't hate me right?

Vicky: *No man…why are you saying this?*

I: Nothing, I'm just saying whatever comes to my mind…

3:19 PM

I: and you seriously are a great guy, dude…

Vicky: *Haha…what makes you say that now?*

I: Nothing…I just wanted to say it J and please take care of Kaavya. She has very few friends…

3:22 PM

Vicky: *Dude, come back to reality. Life is too small. Concentrate on the purpose of your life, and stop thinking too much…*

Look who is explaining me the purpose of my life!

I: Yes, you are right, life is too small. It needs Bournvita! Or Complan…

Vicky: *Hehehe…both are same man…*

I: In my case, life would need steroids… :D but don't forget whatever I'm saying. Take care of Kaavya no matter what…

He didn't reply for a while after this…

3:24 PM

I: You will always take care of Kaavya, reply me…

3:25 PM

Vicky: *Are you going somewhere…?*

I: I don't know, first tell me that you will take good care of Kaavya…

Vicky: *Yes, I will take care of her*

I: :) *bye…*

Vicky: *Hey, listen…*

I: *I'm going…*

Vicky: *You will never do anything wrong. Promise me…At least for Kaavya, she cares a lot about you…*

I was getting irritated, but at the same time my eyes were getting moist. I wanted to cry…

3:30 PM

I: *Everything will be fine if you promise to take care of her, understand? Now should I go?*

Vicky: *Where are you going?*

I: *Wherever! Why should I tell you?*

Vicky: *C'mon, we're friends, if not best friends…*

I: *Hehe.. :) Nowhere…Just wanna pee, urgently!*

Vicky: *Haha…dude, exams are approaching, can you help me with data communications…*

What the hell! I was not even thinking about the upcoming exams. I was actually going to use these exams as an excuse for ending my life!

3:31 PM

I: *Get lost, asshole :P*

Vicky: *saale topper!*

I: *thank u… thank u…I'm going, bye, take care… J*

Vicky: *When will you come back to college?*

How could I tell him, "Mr. MFG, I'm never gonna come back now. You can do whatever you want to do with Kaavya."

I had to execute the plan NOW.

I took the other chair and placed it on top of the bed. I prepared a large noose out of a rope and a bed sheet combined. Sufficient research had made me realise that using just a rope could even result in a broken neck. So I just wanted to strangle to death. Carefully, I tied the hybrid noose to the ceiling fan. It took me a great deal of time. I was already in so much pain that death, by any method, wouldn't hurt now…

Everything was set. It had taken me nearly twenty minutes. I had to conclude everything. I looked at my Gtalk for a while.

I tried to read my conversation with Mr. MFG again…

I would never forget his words, 'One year ago, I did what was good for both of you'…*ASSHOLE*!

I didn't know why I did this, but I asked him again…

3:53 PM
I: Hey…
Vicky: *Yup dude…*

I: One more thing…
Vicky: *What is it?*

I: You still love Kaavya, don't you..? I wanna know the truth, tell me…
Vicky: *Does it make any difference?*

Bloody asshole…Yeah, it wouldn't make any difference. I had prepared everything, now nobody can stop me.

I: Alright, I got it. Does Kaavya love you too?

Although I knew she did...but I wanted to know what he felt. I had no fear of anything...

Vicky: *I don't know about her, but I love her...Leave it man.*

Was this smiley mocking me, or was Kaavya really a player. Only time would tell...

3:58 PM

I: I'm going...bye...

Without waiting for his response, I shut down my laptop, put off the lights, and got ready for a journey to another world...

I stood on my chair; my head was almost reaching the ceiling fan. I looked around my room for the last time. I examined every corner of it. The last eighteen months or so that I had spent in this room were revolving around my head. Those break-ups with 'Ishq', the break-up party, the planning for this great day, everything was visible in front of my eyes.

I took a step further. I put the loop around my neck. I tested the strength of the noose by tugging at it one last time. I wanted to be sure that nothing wrong happened, because this was the last thing I would do in life. This had to be *perfect*. I glanced at my digital watch on the table. It showed 4:09. Without wasting any more time, I tightened the noose. The next instant, I found myself struggling for breath about one foot above the bed in my room. I was hanging from the fan. The digital watch now showed

4:10:03...

4:10:04…

4:10:05…

A few more seconds, I thought, as I tried not to emit any sound from my mouth, even as I was struggling badly for air…

4:10:14…

4:10:15…

My vision was blurring slowly. I could only see the large '4' on the watch. A couple of seconds later, my eyes closed completely…

I was still in pain. My senses were lost now, in real sense. A few more seconds for the 'Heaven Express' to depart… My brain was still thinking, it had not completely died. But that would just take another few minutes…

Yes, my life had ended. But my journey to paradise had just begun…

THE END...?

Rick finished narrating the story and I was speechless; absolutely speechless...

'Ishq' had seriously destroyed him.

"Dude. Nice story. Well narrated. I want to sleep now..." I said. The time was 8 pm. Time for dinner.

"MI...Dude, you didn't tell me the answer to Rony's security question yet..."

I smiled at his curiosity.

"Isn't it obvious? Even Rony is destroyed in love. The answer was 'Reena'..." I revealed.

Rick smiled too. Love can be both a constructive as well as a destructive energy. But I still had one doubt.

"I don't understand why DKP deleted that note?" I said.

"Doesn't it mention about him and Suchi? In 'Last three days of my life'..." Rick explained.

"So what. It mentions about a lot of other people too..." I remarked.

Both of us wondered about it for a while. Actually it was

Rony who had asked DKP to delete the notes citing privacy reasons for Suchi. DKP must have felt that Rony was right. So he deleted the notes and pretended that it was an accident. He, however, didn't know that Rony cared little about the actual implications of his action and only wanted his own name to be removed.

"You know what MI, the perfect word describing Rony is 'Ignoranus'…and that's what I had changed his password to," said Rick.

"What does that mean anyway?" I asked.

"Google it!"

"Right. I'll Google it. But right now I need to sleep…"

"OK, I'll read some other stuff that he has left and you can sleep, after dinner, ok?" said Rick.

We had dinner. He continued to read and I went to sleep.

DESTINIES!

Hey dear friend!
Yes I am talking to you!

The fact that you were able to read this much proves what a true friend of mine you are. Now, although I haven't asked anything about you, I shall tell you something really personal about me. About my *present* life...

You want to listen, right? I'm sure you do.

But before that promise me that you will read it till the end.

C'mon, it isn't a big deal! If you have read it so far, you can read a few more pages, can't you?!

Good...I knew you are my truest friend!

So here goes...

The *Heaven Express* had just entered *Vaikunth Terminus*. The compartments might have been similar to 2A in trains belonging to Indian Railways, or maybe even better, because I have never travelled in an air-conditioned compartment. It wasn't really air-conditioned maybe, but the whole environment inside was quite pleasant. It was a spacious compartment, with just two people in a suite. The other person in the suite might have been about thirty. He was also busy scanning those beautiful interiors. *He sure hasn't seen them before*, I thought.

I got down, and found that the station was really peaceful. One attendant was stationed in front of each compartment. There must have been about two hundred extra-large compartments. We got down, and almost the same number of people entered again. The only difference was that we were all retarded, whereas those who were boarding the train were completely fresh.

"This train runs between Earth and Heaven every half an hour as per Earth time," said a beautiful feminine voice from behind me. I had heard a similar voice somewhere, not long back, but somehow failed to recognize it distinctly. I looked behind me to search for the girl who had such a soothing voice. Our eyes finally met.

"Hi!" she chirped, and ran towards me.

For a moment, I didn't understand what was happening. Her face was familiar, but I failed to remember where I had last seen it. She, on the other hand, didn't seem to have any problems recognizing me.

Coming near me, she immediately hugged me. It was a loving embrace. I put my arms around her in reciprocation and all my miseries melted away in that feeling of oneness.

"Tripti?"

Coming out of the embrace, she looked at me in awe and confusion. Had I recognized her wrongly?

"Aarav! I have been missing you badly baby! It's almost two years since I came here. Everything about this place is perfect except…"

Her eyes were now staring directly into my eyes. She plucked my cheek playfully. Yes, it was Tripti, I had never been so sure before.

"Except…" I said smilingly.

She grinned.

"Except you, my cutie pie…My *shona*…I love you soooo much!" and we were lost in another embrace.

If somebody ever asks you, 'What did you bring, that you will take away?' (After death)

I know the answer, but that's true just for girls.

Tell him that girls have their madness in their soul. It is built into them. They don't have to bring it or take it away.

Seriously, they will never leave their habit of calling you by short and funny names, irrespective of what part of the universe they are taken to…

But I was thoroughly enjoying her love. And the best part was that I didn't have to gather courage and tell her that I loved her. Oh GOD! That would have taken another lifetime!

So here I was, with my dream girl, in a place far better than dreamland.

We came out of that place, and the world outside was magical.

"*Our* home is not far. We can walk," she said.

Not quite sure if 'our' meant just the two of us or something else, I asked, "Where are we going, love…"

"*Muni Naarad Apartments,*" she called out to a flying taxi that had mysteriously appeared from somewhere. It had no wings, no wheels, and looked more or less like the dummy vehicles that one can see in parks, on earth, that is.

Her left arm was around my shoulders, while the right one was over my chest. She slowly caressed me with her right hand, and said, "You have to freshen up and go for a meeting with Indra's secretary. We're heading towards home. You can rest for a while there."

We entered that awful looking taxi which was quite comfortable. It crossed several skyscrapers and bridges swiftly. In less than a minute we landed at our destination. Within seconds of our coming out of that flying vehicle, it disappeared into the air.

"Why didn't you pay?" I got curious about this whole arrangement in heaven.

"You don't have to pay for services that they provide here. Essential services like food, clothing, shelter, and transport are all free."

Amazing! I thought. We entered the building which was guarded by human-like figures that were hovering in the air. On the second floor, we stood in front of a room which had '188/B, Room No. 21' written on it. My mind was now back in action. In *Vaikunth*, they don't have more than nine rooms on a floor and the first number stands for the floor. Seems clean...

The room was no less than a palace. It was perfect for two people. Tripti went ahead to bring some kind of drink for me. I drank it without asking her what it was. I had no option but to trust her completely. She was my dream girl after all.

After a relaxing bath, I asked her, "What is all this meeting with his secretary and all?"

"Nothing, they will just tally your good deeds and bad deeds. If you come clean, you will be given an option to stay here or go back to earth as a human being. Very few people come clean by the way, but I think you will. If you do, they'll allot you some job depending on your capabilities. Otherwise you will have to go back to earth as any living form...and in case someone has absolutely no good deeds, he goes to a place we don't like to talk about."

I didn't want to lose Tripti now. I wanted to stay back here. I didn't want to go back for another life. I didn't want to go back for anything.

♡ ♡ ♡

"May I come in Ma'am?" I tried being polite.

"Yes, Aarav. Please come in," she said sweetly.

I went inside.

"Please sit down. I have studied your life statement carefully. You have performed well in your life on earth. Probably the only sin that you committed was your suicide, but it was all for the good. Would you want to go back for another life term? You get to choose your place of birth this time"

That was a very tempting offer. I could be actually born somewhere in America, maybe Las Vegas. I could spend my life lavishly. Maybe I could just try out how life is, in America. If I didn't like it, I can come back by committing another suicide, without any problems as I already knew everything about it!

But I was sure I didn't want to leave Tripti.

"I'm sure you know what I want, madam," I said, with a smile.

She smiled in return.

"In that case Aarav, you are allotted the job of a chef. You can get the details of it from my assistant. Would you like to have a private residence or any other help?" she asked me.

"I will stay with Tripti. But how can I work as a chef?! I don't know how to cook. By the way, can you tell me more about her friends, Saumya, Divyansh or Vatan?"

She gave me an angry glance, but became subtle and said,

"You will learn how to do your job. I forgot one thing – Boss has told me to deliver a gift to you. It is a very precious ability. Stand up and I will let you have it."

Hesitatingly, I stood up. She closed her eyes, and asked me to close mine. She spoke something that I could not understand, and then asked me to open my eyes.

"You now have the ability to foresee things for people related to you. This ability will remain yours as long as you don't misuse it. Ask for a document of terms and conditions from my assistant. Now you may leave."

"Thank you, madam. I'll talk to your assistant."

I left the room and she became busy with some other files that were lying on her table. After all, she had to attend to several thousand people every hour.

I had got the job of Indra's private hair dresser's chef! I could see what people on earth were doing, plus I can also see the future of my people on earth! Yippie! It is surely a paradise!

I came out of the office, and took full advantage of the free transportation services to observe the beauty of this place.

After an hour I was back home. Tripti was sitting in the balcony, waiting for me.

"So, finally it was worth," she said.

"Yes, it was!" I exclaimed.

I sat beside her. She looked at me and took a deep breath. I continued to stare at her dreamy eyes. I had missed them so much. I couldn't believe I finally had her with me. It was the most enchanting feeling – mysterious, yet completely understood. I felt lost…

She came closer to me and planted a small peck on my cheek. I was arrested by the aroma around her.

I held her soft hands in mine and caressed them.

She came still closer and submitted herself completely to

me. I felt the warmth of her body. I felt her love in my heart. I felt the pain she had gone through, in my absence. She was being freed of all worries.

With closed eyes, we experienced the ultimate joy of the universe. She was silent, completely. I said,

"It was worth"

"Yes...it was..."

She smiled. I smiled in return...

♡ ♡ ♡

Tripti was excited about the whole thing. We spent the rest of the day talking about each other. She was always keeping an eye on me when I was on earth and knew that I would come to her sooner or later. Unlike me, she didn't have the ability to foresee things.

That night, I felt I should try and use my foreseeing capabilities to see what was happening on earth...What I saw was not quite shocking.

Mr. Invisible was busy finding out my notes. He will soon set out to write a full-fledged novel which would based on my notes.

Some seniors were planning out an idea for their new movie – 'The Blessed Cum Cursed Room', in which the room in which I stayed would miraculously become blessed. As per this story, in the coming years, that room would witness all toppers, and all such toppers who came from that room would have no history of love affairs! Another part of the story would be that if anyone tried to occupy that room forcibly or otherwise, just to become 'blessed', he would be cursed with bad luck and bad grades for the rest of his stay at IIT. But since the room is not all that bad, he would also be blessed with a very successful and equivalently useless love life!

Seriously, the idea was great for another short movie. Given their good videography and directional skills, I'm sure this movie would become a huge success.

A MONTH LATER

Kaavya was having a nice time with Vicky. They chatted regularly in private, to make sure that nobody found out what was going on between them. They didn't even go for walks in the campus, but Vicky was certainly happy…

Mr. Invisible cursed me day in and day out for having been a 'rare ICSE student with bad language skills'. He often says, "It's taking more effort than I had realized." But I'm really happy he was making my dream come true. I would have a novel in my name, finally!

Tripti was the best girl I have ever known. The time I spent with her reminded me of the time we had spent on earth. She did better math than me, and often mocked me by saying that she was not even able to give those entrance exams, which was why she couldn't prove herself. I always tell her that it was better if you don't have to go through that painful process of engineering entrance exams! I'm sure most of you will agree with me.

So, everything finally happened for the good…

TWO YEARS LATER

Kaavya got down from *Heaven Express*. There was probably no one waiting for her. The attendant served her a drink. She avoided the drink and ran towards the office of Indra's secretary. I was watching all this from a corner. I had already talked with Lord Indra to let her stay in *Vaikunth*. Recommendations worked here too.

She had committed suicide, for the simple reason that Vicky had deserted her after they had a few physical encounters. I knew Vicky was a bastard. Sorry, I was not supposed to use such a language here. But Vicky's character was more complicated than it appeared.

Kaavya had been given a residence in one of the suburbs of *Vaikunth*, and worked as an assistant of one of those guys who managed the *Heaven Express*. There was no direct conveyance to the place where she stayed from my home. Since I had no personal grudges against anyone, I wished that she lived in peace.

ANOTHER YEAR LATER...

I'm having a great life. It's the year 2015 on earth. April 2015 to be precise...

So congratulations!

You actually survived the end of the world which was supposed to be somewhere in December 2012!

Since Vicky was no longer associated with me, I couldn't tell his future. I should have read the document of terms and conditions well. Anyway, right now he was enjoying himself with another girl named Khushi.

I wonder if Vicky would also commit suicide next. If that were to happen, it would form a perfect plot for a blockbuster Bollywood flick! Believe me!

EPILOGUE...

I woke up, confused. I had just dreamt about Aarav and his life in heaven. I had also peeked into future through Aarav's eyes. Was it really a dream? Or was it a message from Aarav?

I went to the washroom and splashed water over my face. I tried to think. Maybe it really was a message from Aarav. Maybe I shouldn't misuse that information. Maybe I should do something really worth for Aarav...

I came back to my room. Rick was still unaware of my dream.

"So what are we supposed to do of all this information now?" he asked me, scrolling through Aarav's notes.

"Keep it...safe..."

I reached out for my laptop, and set out to right the love story...err, death story of my friend – yes, I had found a friend in Aarav. He wanted to get that account published, and I will do exactly what he wanted...

This page left blank in the memory of Aarav

PERSONS YOU HAVE MET...

Aarav Virani

Aarav was a student at a premier engineering institute in India. He was a juvenile guy, who has excelled academically but failed miserably in love. He was intelligent, and extremely sensitive. He readily accepted the fact that his love interest (and girlfriend) Kaavya was two-timing with him and gave in to the excessive trauma he faced due to her infidelity. He works presently as Indra's (Caretaker of Heaven) private hair dresser's chef at his residence in *Vaikunth* (Heaven) and is in a live-in relationship with his first love – Tripti. He has acquired, as a gift from *Vishnu* (or someone posing as *Vishnu*, as you can't really make out things in heaven too), the ability to foresee things for people related to him.

Kaavya Joshi ('Ishq')

Kaavya was Aarav's batch-mate from the institute, and co-incidentally his girlfriend too. Her name contains all letters from Aarav's name except 'R' which stands for 'Realism'. It also includes the letters 'V' and 'Y' from Vicky's name. She has a great figure, fair complexion, and, not to mention, is extremely intelligent. Although not a completely 'hot' material, she could be considered a fair choice given her academic accolades. As her relationship with Aarav progressesed, he gave her the name 'Ishq' which was 'irritating yet enjoyable', as she felt. She was clear about her emotions for Aarav but assumed that he was someone who could be easily taken advantage of. Her assumption turned out to be unbelievably accurate, and she benefited a lot from Aarav while he was on earth. She was known to be selfish and unforgiving in nature, although Aarav took a lot of time to fully accept this fact.

Vicky Ahuja

Vicky was a total exhibitionist. Right from the first day at IIT, his flirtatious behavior was known to everyone. Vicky constantly tried to woo Kaavya, although he knew about her relationship with Aarav. Kaavya fell for his affections and lost interest in Aarav, which was, apparently, what Vicky actually wanted. He had a fad for his guitar, but people said he didn't really play fairly well. He was referred to as 'Mr. MFG' by Aarav, which was just a way of diluting his frustration.

F4 – Fabulous 4

F4 was a group of four guys who were very close to each other. They were inseparable friends. Aarav was part of this group. Other members were Rohit Bansal aka 'Rony' – an asshole all the way, Dhirendra Kapur aka 'DKP' – a die-hard romantic and Avinash Baruda aka 'Bhalu' – who hadn't yet learnt how to use his brain.

Rony was rich and considered himself the most intelligent person on earth, probably only next to Thomas Edison or something. He played an important role in developing a hazardous arena for Aarav, especially by planning his Break-up party. He was responsible for several blunders in the lives of whole F4 group but things never came to light.

Bhalu had, on numerous occasions, fought for his friends. Although he couldn't think, he was always ready to die for his friends. He had an equally miserable love life, as Aarav, which might be the reason that he was the only one to understand his plight.

Nivedita Raj (Nived)

Nivedita was the ultimate goddess at the female-strived place that the institute campus was. She had a rich, NRI boyfriend. Aarav had a crush on her too, which ultimately resulted in another heart-break. She kept a low profile and maintained very low PDA with her guy. She was the most idolized girl in the history of the campus. Her personal life was inaccessible as she either didn't have a Facebook account, or she had deliberately (and rightly) chosen to keep stalkers at bay!

Suchita Paranjape (Suchi)

Suchita was in a stable relationship with DKP, although she was either unaware of or ignored the fact that DKP was a player, maybe because she was too much smitten by him. Aarav considered her as his sister and close friend, although he once had a crush on her. Not much was known about her behavioral patterns as she loved to spend her time privately and in close proximity of DKP. She once lost a set of about eighty poems composed by Aarav due to which he got highly enraged. Aarav, till date, has been unable to re-compose the original poems completely.

Reena

Reena was Kaavya's friend and Rony's love interest. She was a mysterious figure. She propelled Kaavya's feelings for Vicky, distancing her from Aarav.

Mr. Invisible

Mr. Invisible is a normal student at IIT who does abnormal things. He has very few friends, but they are very true to him. Most of his acts leave no evidence behind, making it difficult for people to even think of suing him. Wait, I think I am talking about myself now! Meh!

Now that you have met all the major characters, why not start from the beginning again…?

ACKNOWLEDGEMENTS

I would like to express my gratitude to the people who have made this novel possible, especially my younger sister who wrote the poem 'Will you be mine' and Rick, who has been very supportive and has always been there whenever I needed him.

The poem 'Safest way to kill me' was written by Aarav himself.

The cover was designed by me with some help from Google and Adobe Photoshop.

I would like to thank everyone who had read whole or part of the book even before it was finalized and gave useful suggestions towards its improvement.

Also, I should thank the publishers for being so patient with me.

I want to thank you, the reader, for buying this book. I hope it didn't disappoint you. Lots of love and take care. May you have a bright future ahead!

www.ingramcontent.com/pod-product-compliance
Lightning Source LLC
Chambersburg PA
CBHW051649260626

47170CB00004B/1417